MEN O' WAR

P.3 – PX7067 / BHC1046 / A752; P.4 – **BHC3762**; P.5 – PY7399 / PAD5628 / PU4026; P.6 – **BHC2889**; P.7 – **BHC3675**; P.8 – BHC2774; P.9 – **BHC0470**; P.10 – PU8209; P.11 – **BHC0492**; P.12 (TOP) – PY0143; P.12 (BOTTOM) – PU0113; P.13 – PU3506; P.14 – 3567; P.15 – BHC2784; P.16 – BHC3602; P.17 – **BHC1782**; P.19 – PY9721; P.21 (TOP) – BHC1046; P.21 (BOTTOM) – B4019-7; P.22 – 7159; P.23 – BHC1045; P.24 – PV5861; P.25 – **BHC1914**; P.26 – 3685; P.29 (TOP) – PAH7444; P.29 (BOTTOM) – PW5807; P.31 (TOP) – ZAZ3859; P.31 (BOTTOM) – E8577; P.32 – E8582; P.33 (TOP) – E1230; P.33 (MIDDLE) – E1186; P.33 (BOTTOM) – E8648; P.34 – PU7765; P.35 – PU3447; P.36 – A765; P.37 – 7301; P.38 – 2033; P.39 – PW3812; P.40 (TOP) – PX8548; P.40 (BOTTOM) – PW3760; P.41 – PU7770; P.42 – PW3762; P.43 – PW4247; P.44 – PW4971; P.45 – PW4203; P.46 – PU3419; P.47 – PW3752; P.50 (TOP) – PW4219; P.50 (BOTTOM)– PY3992; P51 – E8590; P.53 (TOP) – E5497; P.53 (BOTTOM) – PW4969; P.54 – A0626; P.55 – **BHC1950**; P.57 – PU4836; P.59 – PU3772; P.62 – PW3730; P.63 – PU4814; P.65 – PY4903; P.66 – PU3171; P.67 – PW4976; P.69 – PU1358; P.70 – C9949; P.71 – BHC2740; P.72 – BHC0552; P.73 – BHC0471; P.74 – PW3736; P.75 – PW3733; P.78 – C1553; P.79 – A77; P.80 – PW3734; P.81 – PW0456; P.82 – **BHC2554**; P.84 – BHC0480; P.87 – BHC0552; P.89 – PX7067; P.90 – PU4026; P.91 – BHC0499; P.92 – PAD5628; P.96 – 8280; P.97 – PU0157; P.100 – PW2387; P.101 – PU0158; P.102 – PY7339; P.103 (TOP) – PW8407 P.103 (BOTTOM) – PW3445; P.104 – BHC3867; P.105 – PW5794 P.108 – PW3731; P.109 – D4001; P.110 – D5217; P.111 – PW3738; P.112 – 3646; P.113 – D5236; P.114 – PZ0746; P.116 – PU8484; P.117 (TOP) – C8423; P.117 (BOTTOM) – D7562; P120 – **BHC3002**; P121 – **BHC2894**; P.122 – PW2361; P.123 – PY2206; P.124 – A752; P.126 – PZ5425

THIS IS A CARLTON BOOK

Design copyright © Carlton Publishing Group 2003
Text copyright © Peter Goodwin 2003

This edition published in 2003 by Carlton Books Ltd
20 Mortimer Street
London
W1T 3JW

A CIP catalogue for this book is available from the British Library.

ISBN 1-84442-871-0

Project Manager: Stella Caldwell
Editors: Chris Hawkes and Anne McDowall
Managing Art Director: Jeremy Southgate
Picture Research: Eleanor Heron and Lucy Waitt
Production: Lucy Woodhead

Printed in Dubai

I should like to express my sincere thanks to Penny Simpson and Stella Caldwell of Carlton Books for their friendly guidance in producing this work, and likewise to Jeremy Southgate for his superb design. My thanks also extend to Rachel Giles, Eleanor Heron, and Lucy Waitt of the National Maritime Museum, and to my colleague Brian Lavery for his historical expertise and advice. Finally, I very much thank my fiancée, Katy Ball, for her patience and understanding while I was writing the manuscript for *Men O' War*. *Peter Goodwin*

Conversion Tables

Length/distance
1 inch . . . . 2.54 centimetres
1 foot . . . . 30.48 centimetres
1 yard . . . . 0.91 metres
1 mile . . . . 1.6 kilometres
1 fathom (6 feet) . . . 1.829 metres

Weight
1 ounce (1oz) . . . . . 28 grams
1 pound (1lb) . . . . . 453 grams/0.45 kilograms
1 hundredweight (112 lbs) . . . . 50.8 kilograms
1 ton . . . . 1.016 tonnes/1,016 kilograms

Capacity
1 pint . . . . 568 millilitres
1 quart . . . . 1.137 litres
1 gallon . . . . 4.546 litres

Money
1 penny (1d) . . . . . . 0.42 pence
1 shilling (1s) . . . . . . 5 pence
1 guinea (£1.1s) . . . £1.05

Speed
1 knot . . . . 1.15 miles/1.85 kilometres per hour

MEN O' WAR

THE ILLUSTRATED STORY OF LIFE IN NELSON'S NAVY

PETER GOODWIN

Published in association with the National Maritime Museum

CARLTON
BOOKS

NATIONAL
MARITIME
MUSEUM

CONTENTS

"The Buckingham on the Stocks at
Deptford" by John Clevely the Elder.

THE GEORGIAN NAVY FROM 1793 TO 1815

The Georgian navy in which Nelson served remains one of the most cherished periods of naval history, considered by many as the golden era of naval warfare. Mere mention of naval history conjures up images of great wooden sailing warships, sea fights with cannons, muskets and swords, great naval heroes such as Nelson, "Jack Tars" with pigtails, and notorious press gangs, all set against the backdrop of the elegance of Georgian society and the growing impetus of the Industrial Age.

Unfortunately our romantic image of the Georgian navy has been coloured by the distorted accounts from the naval reformers of the 1830s and inadequate research by 19th and early 20th century historians, further embellished by sensation-seeking film and television producers only too willing to please their audiences. In reality, detailed analysis of the primary sources show that Nelson's navy was a highly organized institution supported by a sound provisioning policy. In keeping with the times, it provided an efficient medical and welfare service for its men who, without reasonable food and health, would never have been able to operate the ships for long periods at sea, let alone fight the numerous battles that arose. What is clear is that most seamen employed in the Georgian navy were professional men, highly skilled in the art of seamanship in both its basic sense – handling sails, knotting and splicing ropes, operating the rigging and dealing with both the anchor and other boat work – and its more profound sense – the fundamental art of knowing how to work and survive in every possible situation that arises from the relationship between the natural elements of the sea, wind and sky.

The late 18th and early 19th century was a time of great conflict. Between the Seven Years' War, which started in 1756, and 1815, when Napoleon was finally sent into exile, Britain had spent all but 23 years at war, for the most part with France. The war with France in 1793 was indirectly triggered by the American War of Independence in 1775, when the American colonies revolted against their motherland, England. The catalyst of the American War of Independence, which lasted until 1782, was the Seven Years' War (1756–63). Awakened by the success of the American rebellion and spurred by her own internal unrest and financial difficulties, France commenced her own bloody Revolution in 1789. Few knew at the time that the war resulting from this chaos would develop into a global conflict of unprecedented scale, especially when the fanatical, self-imposed emperor, Napoleon Bonaparte, came into power.

After executing Louis XVI, the deposed king, on 21 January 1793, revolutionary France declared war on Britain, Holland, and Spain 11 days later. The Royal naval fleet, which had formed the bulwark of Britain's defence since Elizabethan times, was mobilized almost immediately and sent to the Mediterranean, the West Indies and other colonies. At the same time,

"Admiral Samuel Hood" by James Northcote. Hood, flying his flag in the Victory, *commanded the British fleet blockading Toulon 1793-94.*

ships forming the Channel fleet blockaded French naval ports such as Brest and Rochefort, while other vessels were deployed to escort the great mercantile fleets of East and West Indiamen as they sailed forth to their respective overseas destinations. On land, the naval press gangs vigorously recruited men to supplement the undermanned ships hurriedly being completed within the dockyards to meet demands of war. Nelson, having spent five years on shore, left his wife Frances at their home in Burnham Thorpe, to take command of the 64-gun ship *Agamemnon*, which had been refitting at Chatham. Following orders, he sailed for the Mediterranean to join Admiral Hood's fleet which was blockading the French naval port of Toulon.

Although distinguished sea fights highlighted the next

22 years, the ships spent the majority of their time undertaking wearisome tasks, such as blockading enemy ports and escorting convoys. The first notable sea victory came in 1794, when Admiral Howe intercepted a vast grain fleet and its naval convoy returning to France some 100 miles south-southwest of Ireland. Because France was dependent on American grain, capturing these ships was important. Intercepting the enemy on 1 June, Howe gave battle to his adversary Admiral Villaret Joyeuse. However, although six French ships were captured or sunk, the grain ships got away. This battle, which came to be known as the "Glorious First of June", greatly boosted naval confidence.

By the end of August 1793, royalist French forces in Toulon had been overwhelmed by a brilliant artilleryman named Napoleon Bonaparte and the ensuing naval battles proved indecisive. This destroyed any real hopes of Britain securing a bridgehead and invading France from the southeast. In 1794, Nelson was consigned to take a small squadron of ships to Corsica to support loyalists against the invading French revolutionary forces; the main objective however was to establish a secure base for the Mediterranean fleet. After landing guns, seamen and marines from the *Agamemnon*, Nelson placed the town of Bastia under siege; the French garrison holding the town finally capitulated on 23 May. In the subsequent battle at Calvi on 12 July, Nelson was

"The Battle of the Glorious First of June" by Phillipe Jacques de Loutherbourg, showing Howe's flagship Queen Charlotte *engaging the French* Bretagne. *This painting captures the chaos of a sea fight.*

Napoleon Bonaparte: an engraving after Delpech.

struck in the right eye by gravel that had been blown up from a nearby bursting shell on the defensive ramparts. Although he did not actually lose his eye, as most people believe, the injury did leave him blind in his right eye.

On 19 September 1794, Hood's command of the Mediterranean fleet was succeeded by Admiral Hotham. Hotham's command, other than a rather indecisive engagement off Genoa on 14 March 1795, during which Nelson took his little 64-gun *Agamemnon* into action against the 80-gun *Ca Ira*, proved to be defensive and ineffective, and as a result the French gained the upper hand in the war in the Mediterranean. Inevitably Hotham was replaced by Admiral Sir Hyde Parker who was himself relieved by the more diligent leader, Admiral Sir John Jervis (pronounced Jervis, and not "Jarvis" as is commonly believed) on 21 December 1795. In 1796, Nelson, who came to be much respected by Jervis, was promoted to the rank of Commodore and was transferred into the 74-gun ship *Captain* on 11 June. His previous command *Agamemnon*, which had been built in 1781, was sent home for a much-needed refit. In the meantime, France had taken control on all fronts, and with Genoa and Leghorn closing their ports to the British, and with Spain entering the war on the side of France in October 1796, the British fleet, through lack of bases, was compelled to quit the Mediterranean. Last to leave was Nelson, who, having been given the frigate *La Minerve*, helped with the evacuation of British forces based on Elba in December 1796. Nelson rejoined the British fleet, now laying off Gibraltar, in February 1797, bringing news that he had sighted a large Spanish fleet.

Jervis, flying his flag on the 100-gun *Victory*, immediately ordered his 15 ships of the line and five frigates to sea; Nelson rejoined the *Captain*. The Spanish fleet, commanded by Admiral Don José de Cordova, comprised nearly twice the number of line of battleships, which were escorting a large convoy carrying a consignment of mercury, essential for the refining of silver in the New World. Just before noon on 14 February 1797, the two fleets engaged in what was later called the battle of Cape St. Vincent, after the closest headland on the Iberian coast. As the foremost British ships manoeuvred to get abreast of their opponents, Nelson, stationed towards the rear, saw that the leading Spanish ships had an easy path to escape. To prevent this, he broke out of the formal "line of battle" to cut off their line of retreat, and exposed the *Captain* to intense gunfire in the process. Jervis quickly ordered the ships behind Nelson to follow and give support. By this time Nelson had drawn his 74-gun ship alongside the 80-gun *San Nicolas* and led a boarding party on board the Spanish vessel. After capturing her, he crossed over to the 112-gun ship *San Josef* that lay partially damaged nearby. With five vessels captured and others surrendering, Jervis had gained a great victory. Jervis was given an Earldom and Nelson was created a Knight of the Bath.

However, all was not well in the fleet; seamen serving in the Royal Navy had not received a wage rise for over 100 years. This, together with inflation, deteriorating conditions and grievances about allowances, created much discontent – a discontent that spread through to the lower decks of the men o' war forming the Channel fleet. Petitions for improvement sent to the Admiralty were ignored and eventually, after refusing to weigh anchor, the seamen at Spithead mutinied on 15 April 1797. This was not the violent occurrence often associated with a mutiny, but a well-organized and dignified mass demonstration instigated by literate men. Although their officers may have ceased to control their ships, marks of respect towards the officers were upheld. Discipline likewise was fully maintained and any crime received its due punishment. By May, just as it seemed as though most grievances had been resolved, and after an improvement in pay had been offered, a second mutiny started on the *Nore* led by Richard Parker. On this occasion however, the delegates of the mutiny were not to be appeased by the Admiralty and it was quelled with swift reprisal: Parker and his collaborators were hanged. Wary of further unrest, discipline from that point on was maintained more vigorously.

The success of the battle of Cape St. Vincent, and Admiral Duncan's victory at the battle of Camperdown against the Dutch fleet allied to France in October 1797, greatly improved morale, and the cohesion of the navy was restored. In 1798, the British fleet, led by Nelson in the 74-gun ship *Vanguard*, re-entered the Mediterranean to support the Neapolitan struggle against invading revolutionary forces. Learning that Napoleon, who was now in a position of considerable power, intended to invade Egypt and move east to take Britain's possessions in India, Nelson sailed from Naples in the *Vanguard* to seek out the French fleet, commanded by Admiral De Brueys, carrying the Grand Army. Nelson finally found the enemy anchored in Abu-Kir Bay, east of Alexandria, on 1 August. Immediately ordering his ships to clear for action, Nelson planned to attack from both sides, taking half his squadron into the shallow waters between the land and the anchored fleet. This unexpected plan caught the French completely unawares. The battle started in the late afternoon and continued into the

"Nelson boarding the San Josef *at the Battle of Cape St. Vincent, 14 February 1797", by George Jones. Having taken this Spanish 3-decker ship, Nelson, using this captured vessel as a "patent boarding bridge" then crossed over to successfully capture the* San Nicolas.

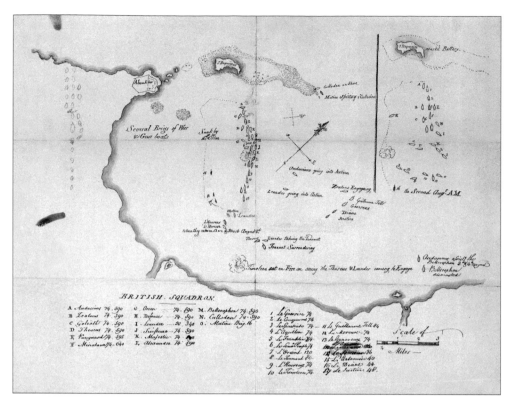

BRITISH SQUADRON.

A	Audacious	74 . 590	G	Orion	74 . 590	M	Bellerophon 74. 590
B	Zealous	74 . 590	H	Defence	74 . 590	N	Culloden 74 . 590
C	Goliath	74 . 590	I	Leander	50 . 340	O	Mutine Brig 16
D	Theseus	74 . 590	K	Majestic	74 . 590	
E	Vanguard	74 . 595	L	Alexander	74 . 590	
F	Minotaur	74 . 640				

1	Le Guerrier 74
2	Le Conquerant 74
3	Le Spartiate 74
4	L'Aquilon 74
5	Le Franklin 84
6	Le Souveraine 74
7	L'Orient 120
8	Le Tonnant 80
9	L'Heureux 74
10	Le Timoleon 74

11	Le Guillaume Tell 84
12	Le Mercure 74
13	Le Genereux 74
14	La Serieuse 36
15	La Artemise 40
16	La Diane 44
17	La Justice 48

Above: A map of the Battle of the Nile in the Bay of Abu-Kir, 1 August 1798, by Nicholas Pocock. Listed below are the British ships of Nelson's squadron and the French ships captured or destroyed.

Right: "Admiral Francis Paul Count de Brueys" by Alexandre Lacauchie. De Brueys, who commanded the French fleet at the battle of the Nile, was killed before his flagship, the great 120-gun L'Orient, blew up.

night, during which time De Brueys' massive 120-gun flagship *L'Orient* caught fire and blew up with overwhelming loss of life, including that of the noble French admiral. With few French ships escaping capture, this battle effectively secured Britain's prestige in the Mediterranean and thwarted Napoleon's ambitions, forcing him to take his Grand Army north to invade the Levant and the port of Acre.

In the meantime, Nelson divided his forces: part of the fleet was sent to blockade the French at Malta and part to the Levantine coast, while Nelson himself sailed to Italy to support the King of Naples against the invading revolutionary army. The British squadron operating in the Levant was placed under the very able leadership of Sir Sydney-Smith who, landing a large force of marines and seamen, lay siege to Acre. His attack and subsequent defence of the city was so successful that the Grand Army was obliged to retire south back to Egypt, where a later attack in 1801, supported by the British Navy, Lord Keith and Abercrombie, finally dashed French hopes of taking India and retaining Egypt.

The year 1798 proved to be the turning point of the war in Britain's favour. The next major campaign, inspired by the Tsar Paul I of Russia, was to break the alliance between Denmark, Prussia, Sweden and Russia. Fully supported by Napoleon, this "Armed Neutrality of the North" – as this new coalition was named – had been formed to prevent British warships stopping and searching Danish and Russian merchant vessels and confiscating the cargoes intended for French ports. For Napoleon this had two advantages, for not only could the coalition break the British blockade of France, it could also prevent the British Navy from receiving much-needed supplies from the Baltic states. These important stores comprised flax, hemp, tar, turpentine and timber, without which British naval and merchant ships could not refit. To break the embargo, a large fleet, commanded by Admiral Sir Hyde Parker, with Nelson second in command, sailed from Yarmouth in March 1801 with the objective of bringing each of the respective naval fleets to heel. Reaching Copenhagen on 2 April, Nelson moved in to crush the Danish fleet protecting the city, but the Danes put up a formidable defence. The battle transformed into a prolonged and indecisive gunnery match with ever-rising casualties on both sides. Realizing the futility of the circumstances, Nelson resorted to diplomacy, persuading the Crown Prince of Denmark to denounce Danish support of the coalition and his country's collaboration with France. The British Navy then sailed further into the Baltic to blockade the Swedes at Karlskrona and the Russian Navy anchored at their base at Revel, today Tallinn in Estonia. The blockade, together with the recent assassination of Tsar Paul I on 11 March, led to the disintegration of the northern alliance.

Napoleon's threat of invading England was averted by the Channel squadrons led by Nelson and, by the end of 1801, both Britain and France, having exhausted their finances, were forced to end the conflict. After nine years of fighting, the Treaty of Amiens was signed on 27 March 1802 bringing a close to the French Revolutionary War. In August, Napoleon became the First Consul of France. The fragile peace did not prevail and on 16 May 1803 war with France reopened, and with it the threat of an invasion by Napoleon. Four days later Nelson sailed from Portsmouth in the frigate *Amphion* to take command of the Mediterranean fleet; his intended flagship, the 100-gun *Victory*, followed later. His main objective was to blockade the French fleet at Toulon.

On 18 May 1804 Napoleon was proclaimed emperor by the French Senate and in December was crowned sovereign of France by Pope Pius VII. In the new year Napoleon embarked upon his great plan for the invasion of Britain by amassing his Grand Army at Boulogne. Napoleon's intention was to support these invasion forces with a combined Franco-Spanish fleet, but this meant having to take control of the English Channel from the Royal Navy. In order to effect his grandiose scheme he needed to draw the British ships from the Channel. He therefore ordered Admiral Pierre Villeneuve to break out into the Atlantic and attack British colonies in the West Indies, hoping that this diversion would leave the English Channel virtually free for the Franco-Spanish fleet to support the invasionary forces.

With Austria, Russia and Sweden forming the Third Coalition with Britain against France in May 1805, Napoleon found himself threatened on two fronts. And while he maintained that the invasion of Britain was the key to breaking this alliance, his situation had become more exasperated. While some French squadrons did evade the British blockades and managed to escape out of harbour in accordance with Napoleon's designs, the success of his plans foundered because of two factors: Nelson's dogged pursuit of Villeneuve's fleet across the Atlantic and, more importantly, the tight blockade of the French ports on the Atlantic coast and English Channel by Admiral Cornwallis.

Sir William Smith, who commanded the 74-gun Theseus *at Acre.*

The gamble to draw the British fleet westward failed and, although Villeneuve's fleet was partially engaged by Admiral Calder in July 1805, Villeneuve disobeyed his emperor and took his combined fleet south to Cadiz rather than north into the Channel as ordered. This action, together with the failure of other squadrons getting beyond the iron grip of Cornwallis' blockade, forced Napoleon to abandon the invasion of Britain and march his Great Army encamped at Boulogne eastward to fight a new campaign against Austria. Meantime, the British fleet remained outside

Cadiz, waiting to strike. Issuing new orders, Napoleon directed Villeneuve to sail with his combined fleet for the Mediterranean to support the new campaign against Austria and Russia. This gave Nelson and Admiral Collingwood, his second-in-command, the perfect opportunity to destroy the main force of enemy ships. Devising a plan – referred to as the "Nelson Touch" – Nelson intended to attack the combined fleet from 90 degrees in three columns in an attempt to confuse the enemy. Nelson altered his plan on discovering that there were less available ships than he had hoped and decided to attack in two columns rather than three. On 19 October his inshore squadrons sent news that the combined fleet was preparing to sail the next day from Cadiz for the Straits of Gibraltar.

Villeneuve's squadron comprised 33 ships of the line and six frigates; Nelson's smaller force was made up of 27 line of battleships, four frigates, a schooner and a cutter. In the early hours of Monday 21 October, Villeneuve, who had been progressing on a south-easterly course towards the Straits of Gibraltar, turned his fleet 180 degrees to give battle. As the two fleets converged, some 15 miles southwest of Cape Trafalgar, at 11.25 a.m., Nelson hoisted his famous signal, "England expects that every man will do his duty", after which he telegraphed signal No. 16: "Engage the enemy more closely". Battle commenced just before noon, with Collingwood in the *Royal Sovereign* breaking the enemy line at the rear. Half an hour later, Nelson, leading the windward column, came up with the van of the enemy in the *Victory* and fired a devastating broadside into Villeneuve's flagship, *Bucentaure*, before colliding with and engaging the French 74-gun *Redoutable*, commanded by Captain Jean-Jacques Lucas. At the height of the fighting around 1.15 p.m., Nelson was shot by a musket ball fired from the mizzen top of the *Redoutable* and was carried below. The ferocious battle continued all afternoon. Superior gunnery, tactics and the condition of the English seamen however won the day and by 4 p.m. some 17 ships had been taken. Around 4.30 p.m. Nelson finally died of his wound, but not before receiving news that the battle had been won. At 5.30 p.m. the French vessel *Achille* blew up, bringing the total of ships captured or destroyed to 18, a figure that included the great Spanish 136-gun ship, *Santisima Trinidad*. Nelson's victory off Cape Trafalgar ensured that Napoleon no longer had the naval capacity to support any potential invasion of either England or any other country. Spain would never be a force of maritime strength again, while France could do nothing more than keep her remaining ships in harbour.

In the spring of 1806, Admiral Thomas Duckworth defeated a French force off St. Domingo in the West Indies. This last fleet action effectively re-established British supremacy in the Caribbean. From this point of the war, most naval actions were fought with minor squadrons and frigates. In 1807, Napoleon invaded Portugal and began to assert his power over Spain, resulting in the Spanish changing their alliance to Britain the following year. The year 1807 also saw the incident concerning the impressment of American seamen from the USS *Chesapeake* – it was an incident that would lead to war with the United States in 1812. In 1808, the role of the British Navy was mainly centred towards supporting the Peninsular War, by transporting army battalions commanded by the Duke of Wellington to Portugal. In the north, the navy, under Admiral Saumarez flying his flag in the *Victory*, commenced the Baltic campaign.

During this phase of the Napoleonic War much of the fighting was left to squadrons of frigates deployed in various stations – the most notable being by William Hoste commanding the *Amphion* in the Adriatic. After spending some two years supporting Italian loyalists and harassing enemy shipping and coastal installations off the Dalmation coast, Hoste's great moment came at the battle of Lissa on 11 March 1810. With only four frigates, he took on a French force of ten vessels. As he closed with the enemy he flew the signal "Remember Nelson".

In 1812, the inevitable conflict with the United States of America began, in which the much more heavily armed American 44-gun frigates defeated a number of British frigates. The most significant incident of the war saw the destruction of the frigate *Java*, blown up during her action with the *Constitution*. This war, together with the war against France, ended in 1814 and brought to an end a period of conflict that had lasted for the best part of 21 years. During this time the Georgian navy had attained full mastery of the seas, achieving this lofty status as a result of intricate organization, its rigid discipline and the welfare of the men that served in the men o' war. The much-welcomed period of "Pax Britannia" had begun.

"Captain Sir William Hoste" by Samuel Lane. A Norfolkman like Nelson, he commanded the frigate Amphion *during operations off the Dalmation coast.*

SHIPS AND WEAPONRY

When war with France recommenced on 16 May 1803, great efforts were made to mobilize and increase the size of the British fleet. By the end of the year, the entire British fleet, including all manner of warships, transports and troopships, comprised some 871 vessels, amounting to about 800,500 tons of shipping. This figure was made up of 181 line of battleships, 394 frigates, sloops, brigs and cutters, 119 armed-support craft, such as gun-boats, and 177 transports and other kinds of support vessels.

Opposite page: "The Royal George off Deptford" by John Cleveley the Elder. Launched at Woolwich in 1756, this 100-gun first-rate ship accidentally foundered with a loss of some 1,000 lives at Spithead in August 1782.

Below: "The Royal Dockyard at Chatham" by Joseph Farington. Looking east, this view shows the building slips at the centre where Nelson's Victory was constructed.

The larger fighting ships were divided into six separate rates – first, second, third etc. – according to the number of guns carried. The concept of "rating" ships, which originated in the 17th century, also influenced the pay differentials between captains in command of ships of different rates: the larger the ship, the higher the rate of pay. The first-, second- and third-rate ships, generally referred to as either "ships of the line" or "line of battleships", and later simply "liners", were vessels that had sufficient firepower to fight in the line of battle and equally were strong enough to sustain enemy gunfire. Carrying their ordnance on two or three decks, their armament comprised either 32-, 24-, 18- or 12-pounder guns, the lighter guns being placed higher in the

The British Fleet, 31 December 1803

Rate or type	Guns	Decks	Number
First	100–120	3	10
Second	90–98	3	19
Third	80–84	2	13
Third	74	2	91
Third	60–64	2	48
TOTAL line of battleships			**181**
Fourth	50–56	2	22
Fourth	44	2	2
Fifth	44	1	16
Fifth	40	1	7
Fifth	38	1	44
Fifth	36	1	46
Fifth	32	1	51
Sixth	20–28	1	41
Ship-sloops and brig-sloops	14–18	1	153
Cutters	4–14	1	12
TOTAL frigates and "cruisers"			**394**
Bomb vessels	8 and 2 mortars	-	18
Fireships	14	-	6
Armed schooners	6–12	-	22
Gun-brigs	10–14		47
Gun-boats	1–4	-	24
Armed barges	1–4	-	2
TOTAL armed support craft			**119**
Armed transports and troopships	14		51
Storeships and tenders		-	15
Advice boats		-	2
Sloop on an expedition of discovery	-	-	1
Hospital ships		-	3
Yachts, royal and large			7
Receiving ships, hulks, hoys, and miscellaneous		-	98
TOTAL miscellaneous vessels			**177**
TOTAL VESSELS IN FLEET			**871**

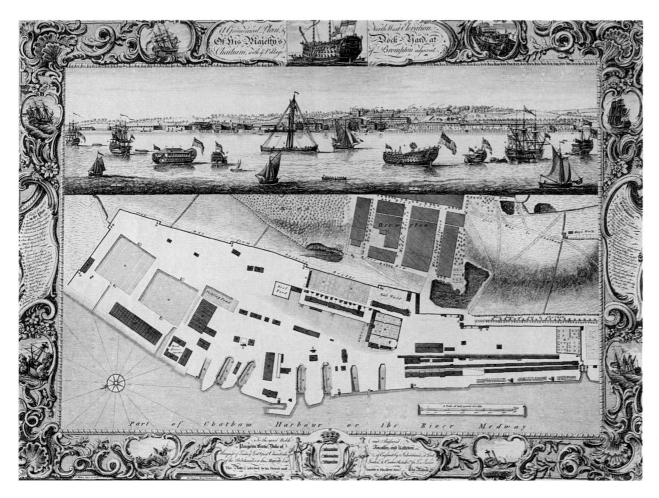

Prospect and plan of Chatham Dockyard showing the two great mast ponds to the north (left), building docks and dockyards officer's houses centre, while south (right) lay the long rope walk and main store houses.

Ships Under Construction, 31 December 1803

Rate or type	Guns	Decks	Number
First	120	3	3
Second	98	3	4
Third	74	2	9
Fifth	36–38	1	13
Sloops	14–18	1	28
Yachts	-	-	2
TOTAL frigates and "cruisers"			**59**

ship. At the same time, a further 59 ships were being built to increase the combat effectiveness of the fleet and to supersede vessels that had become obsolete.

First-Rate Ships

In 1803 there were only ten first-rate ships, with a further three in the process of being built. Armed with between 100 and 120 guns, these ships were manned with a crew of between 850 and

875 men. They averaged at about 190 feet in length on the lower gun deck, 52 feet in breadth, had a draught of 22 to 24 feet and a tonnage of around 2,200 tons. When rigged, armed and stored, their displacement, including the weight of their crew, could exceed 3,500 tons. Their general armament comprised 32-pounder guns on their lower gun deck, 24-pounders on the middle gun deck and 12-pounders on their upper gun deck and quarter deck, supplemented with carronades. A three-decked ship of 100 guns, such as Nelson's *Victory*, could deliver a devastating broadside weight of over half a ton of iron shot.

The amount of timber used to construct these ships comprised about 6,000 loads, which equates to 300,000 cubic feet of timber, of which 90 per cent would have been oak. This amount of timber – the equivalent of about 6,000 trees – would have been extracted from some 100 acres of woodland. These figures relate to the initial quantity of timber required before it was converted into the designed components that formed the construction of the ship. Because of their size and cost to maintain, few first-rate ships were built. Although these vessels were relatively slow due to their size – they had an average speed of seven to eight knots – if designed with good underwater lines, some, such as the *Victory*, could attain a top speed of ten to 11 knots under special conditions. With commodious cabin space aft for an admiral, these ships were usually used as flagships.

Second-Rate Ships

Carrying between 90 and 98 guns on three decks, these ships were effectively a less costly class of ship than the first-rate, three-decked warship. Being smaller, their armament comprised 32-pounder guns on their lower gun deck, 18-pounders on the middle gun deck and 12-pounders on their upper gun deck and quarter deck. Carrying less ordnance, their crew comprised 750 men. Like the first-rate ships, these would also be used as flagships.

Third-Rate Ships

This class of ship, carrying between 64 and 84 guns on two decks, formed the main body of the "line of battle" fleet. In 1803, there were 152 third-rate ships, of which nine were 84-gun ships, 96 were 74-gun ships, and 36 were 64-gun ships. The 74-gun ships were the most effective design and size. Armament comprised 24- or 32-pounder guns on the lower gun deck, 24- or 18-pounders on the upper gun deck and nine- or 12-pounders on the quarter deck, according to the size of the vessel. Depending on both class and armament, the crew size varied between 550 and 700 men. The average 74-gun ship was about 170 feet in length on the lower gun deck, 48 feet in breadth, had a draught of 20 to 22 feet and a tonnage of around 1,670 tons. A two-decked ship of 74 guns, such as Nelson's *Theseus,* could deliver a devastating broadside weight of about 780 pounds of iron shot. The amount of timber used to construct a 74-gun ship was about 2,410 loads, which equates to 120,500 cubic feet of timber before conversion. This amount of timber, 90 per cent of which was oak, the equivalent of about 2,400 trees, would have been cut down from some 70 acres of woodland. Although occasionally used as flagships, these ships could either form part of the battle fleet, or, because they were faster, could operate with smaller squadrons. Running before the wind, the 74-gun ship could attain a speed of 11 knots.

Fourth-Rate Ships

Carrying between 44 and 60 guns of lesser calibre, these small, two-decked ships were too lightly armed to stand in the "line of battle" and were therefore invariably employed as convoy escorts, used to undertake naval operations in shallow waters, where larger ships with a deeper draught could not sail, and reconnaissance duties. These ships were about 146 feet long on the gun deck,

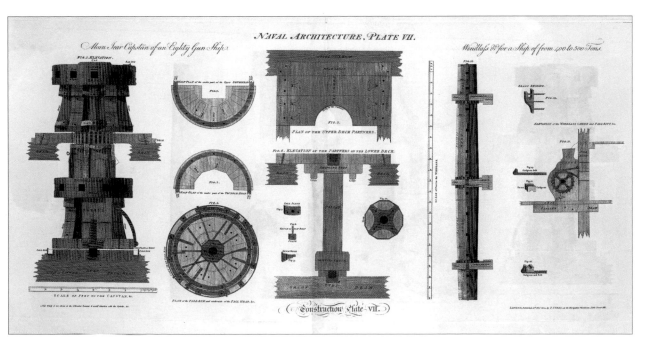

Above: The 64-gun third-rate ship St Albans *being floated out of the dock at Deptford; painting by John Cleveley the Elder.*

Left: Plan showing the construction of a capstan for an 80-gun ship, left, and a windlass, used in smaller ships, right.

41 feet in breadth, drew about 18 feet of water and weighed about 1,050 tons. The average speed for this size of ship was between eight and nine knots. The complement of a 50-gun ship would have been around 350 men and 425 in a 60-gun ship. Limited in their capability, by 1803 most of the 64 ships covering this class were virtually obsolete remainders from the American War of Independence and earlier. Therefore, by 1805, many of these vessels had been transformed into troopships or had been converted for other requirements. One example is the 44-gun *Janus*, which was renamed *Dromedary* in 1788 and converted into a 24-gun storeship and, in 1800, was deployed in the West Indies as a troopship. The 50-gun *Bristol*, in which Nelson served as a lieutenant in 1778, was converted into a prison ship at Chatham in 1794 until it was finally broken up in 1810.

Fifth-Rate Ships

This class of ships comprised the heavier types of frigates, carrying between 32 and 44 guns of various calibre mounted on a single gun deck. Like the fourth rates, these vessels were too lightly armed and too lightly built to stand in the "line of battle". Being fast cruisers, capable of speeds of between 12 and 14 knots, frigates generally operated independently from the fleet, undertaking multifarious roles such as working as part of an inshore squadron, reconnaissance of enemy ports, scouting, working as the "eyes of the fleet", as Nelson dubbed them, or were involved with more clandestine work. Alternatively, they were often deployed as convoy escorts. A typical 38-gun

Sail plan of a three-masted "ship rigged" vessel showing square sails only. On the bowsprit, projecting beyond the front of the frigate, is the spritsail and sprit topsail. From top to bottom of the foremast, the sails are the fore royal, fore topgallant, fore topsail, and four course. Sails on the main and mizzen are similarly named with the appropriate prefix. The aftermost sail set on a gaff yard is the spanker. The additional sails each side on the fore and main masts are studding sails set in lights winds for extra speed.

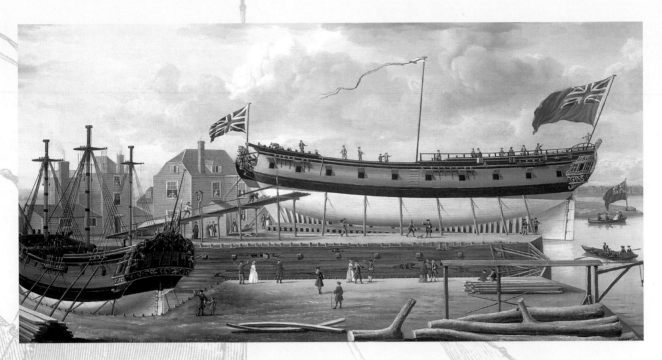

*A 24-gun sixth-rate
frigate on the stock ready
for launch. This painting,
by John Cleveley the Elder,
clearly shows the specially
constructed launching
cradle.*

frigate of the *Amphion* class, designed in 1796, had a length on the deck of 144 feet, a breadth of
38 feet, a draught of about 15 feet and weighed 920 tons. The armament on these vessels
comprised 18-pounders on the main deck, two six-pounder guns and eight 24-pounder carronades
on the quarter deck, and two six-pounders and two 24-pounder carronades on the forecastle. This
gave a single broadside weight of 300 pounds. Their complement comprised 254 men. Before
conversion, some 1,590 loads of timber were used in constructing a 38-gun ship, equating to
about 79,500 cubic feet of timber taken from about 37 acres of woodland. The slightly smaller
32-pounder frigates generally carried 12-pounder guns on their main deck. Although there were
164 fifth-rate frigates in the fleet by 1803 – a considerable number – Nelson claimed that there
were never enough of these most useful vessels.

Sixth-Rate Ships

This class of ship comprised the smaller frigates carrying between 20 and 28 guns of various
calibre mounted on a single gun deck. Like their larger counterparts, these vessels never fought in
the "line of battle" but, being nimble and capable of speeds of between 12 and 14 knots, and
under exceptional conditions as much a 16 knots, operated independently. Besides undertaking
duties of scouting, escorting convoys and working close inshore, these vessels also undertook
policing roles to stop and search neutral ships entering or leaving enemy ports; they were also
deployed as convoy escorts. Most of the sixth-rate frigates still in service in 1803 were built before
the American War of Independence. The typical 28-gun frigate of the *Mermaid* class, designed in
1760, had a length on the deck of 124 feet, a breadth of 33 feet 6 inches and a draught of about
14 feet and weighed 615 tons. The armament on these vessels comprised nine-pounders on the
main deck and four three-pounder guns on the quarter deck plus 12 half-pounder swivel guns,
giving a single broadside weight of 114 pounds. The complement comprised 200 men, while that

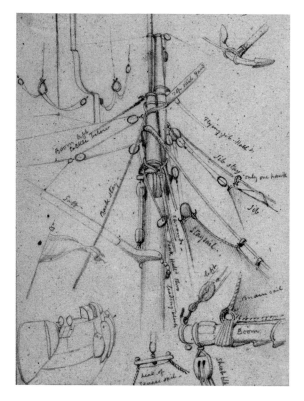

Working sketch showing various details of the pulley blocks that provided mechanical advantage to the rigging.

of a 24-gun ship was 160 men. Before conversion, some 1,267 loads of timber were used in constructing a 28-gun ship, equating to about 63,350 cubic feet of timber taken from about 29 acres of woodland. In total, there were only 41 sixth-rate frigates in service in 1803.

Ship-Sloops and Brig-Sloops

Carrying between 14 and 18 guns, these smaller vessels undertook similar duties to the sixth-rate frigates, but unlike their larger counterparts they rarely used their guns in sustained action. Their armament was mainly used for defensive rather than offensive needs. The difference between ship-sloops and brig-sloops lay in the manner in which the vessel was rigged: ship-sloops were three-masted "ship-rigged" vessels; the brig-sloops were two-masted, "brig-rigged" vessels, i.e. foremast, mainmast and bowsprit only. Ship-sloops – generally 100 feet in length, 27 feet in breadth and with a weight of some 320 tons – carried their main armament of six-pounder guns on one main deck, 12-pounder carronades on their quarter deck and forecastle, and had a complement of 125 men. Other vessels of this type were flush decked – without a quarter deck or forecastle – and carried 32-pounder carronades. In 1803 their were 153 sloops in service, of which 64 per cent were ship-sloops. The brig-sloops, which were slightly smaller in size and flush decked, carried similar types of armament.

Cutters

These were single-masted ships carrying a vast sail area which made them highly suitable for quick raids inshore, coastal defence, reconnaissance and transferring despatches from the fleet either to shore or to other squadrons. Mounting four to 14 three-, four-, or six-pounders on an open deck, or alternatively 12-pounder carronades, these vessels had a crew of between 60 and 80 men. This type of vessel was so successful in design that it was readily adopted by the Customs and Excise men for use as revenue cutters. By 1803, only 12 remained in service. These cutters, together with the six separate rates, the sloops, brigs, bomb vessels, fireships, and the gun brigs, made up what was termed the "cruisers" of the fleet, which in 1803 totalled some 575 vessels.

Bomb Ships

Used mainly to bombard coastal installations, these stout vessels were purpose built to take the weight and recoil forces generated from firing heavy mortars. Their armament comprised one 13-inch and one ten-inch mortar mounted midships on rotating carriages. These fired spherical

explosive shells a maximum distance of 4,100 yards (two and a half miles). When packed with explosive, these shells weighed some 210 pounds. Alternatively, these mortars could fire lethal incendiaries called "carcasses". For defensive requirements, they carried eight four- or six-pounder carriage guns. Originally designed with a two-masted ketch rig, by 1803 all bomb vessels were ship rigged which provided a better balanced rig. Usually accompanied by a tender carrying a contingent of the Royal Marine Artillery who fired the mortars, this ship-type carried a standard crew of 65 to sail the vessel. Bomb vessels were used during Nelson's attack on Copenhagen in 1801 and during the second attack in 1807. When not used as a bomb ship, these vessels could be readily converted into a sloop by removing the mortars, in which case the crew was increased by 50 men. These vessels were 95 to 110 feet in length, 27 to 29 feet in breadth and varied between 300 and 400 tons, according to their class type. In 1803 there were 18 bomb vessels in service.

"The Royal Dockyard at Plymouth Looking East" by Nicholas Pocock. Like Portsmouth, this dockyard was greatly expanded in the late 17th century to meet the demands of war with France.

Fire Ships

Frequently used during the 17th century to set fire to fleets, there were only six fire ships in service in 1803. Specially designed to contain a high quantity of incendiaries, these ships carried about 14 light guns for defensive requirements and a crew of no more that 45 men.

Armed Schooners

These fast, two-masted vessels were generally employed for inshore work and for carrying despatches. They would vary between 75 and 100 feet in length, were 25 feet in breadth and weighed 126 tons. Carrying between six and 12 guns or carronades, they were manned by a crew of about 60 men. The most famous schooner employed was the *Pickle*, commanded by Lieutenant Lapenotoire, who brought back the first news to Britain of Nelson's victorious defeat of the combined Franco-Spanish fleet off Cape Trafalgar, as well as Admiral Collingwood's despatches and the sad news of Lord Nelson's death.

Gun Brigs

Designed for inshore work, coastal defence and carrying out attacks up river estuaries, this class of vessel could be used for rowing as well as sailing. Their maximum length was 75 feet, their

"Prospect and plan of Plymouth Dockyard" showing the rope house and great quadrilateral storehouse (right) and the dockyards officers' houses above the great basin and docks (centre).

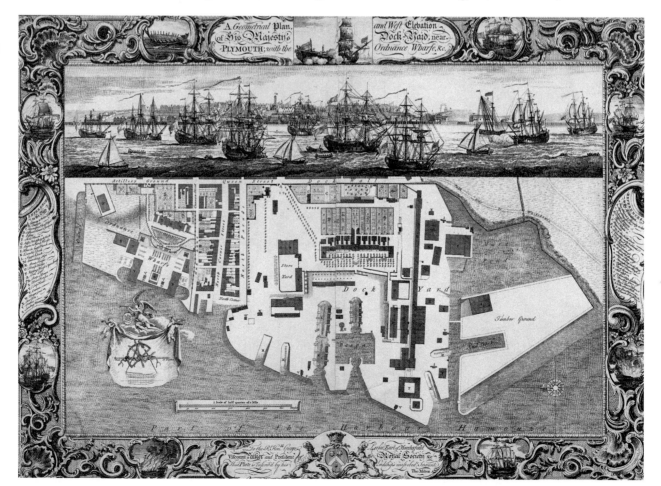

breadth 21 feet, and they weighed 146 tons. Their armament, which varied from ten to 14 guns, consisted of 18-pounder carronades and two 24-pounder chase guns. The maximum crew was a total of 50 men.

Gun-boats and Armed Barges

Designed for making attacks up river estuaries, this class of vessel would have been towed by larger vessels and then rowed or sailed to the point of attack. They carried one to four pieces of ordnance of 12-, 18- or 24-pounder standard guns on slide carriages or similar calibre carronades. In 1803, there were 24 gun-boats and two armed barges.

The other vessels that made up the rest of the fleet – 177 in all – comprised 51 armed transports and troopships, 15 storeships and tenders, two advice boats, three hospital ships, one sloop on an expedition of discovery and seven large yachts, of which one was used as a Royal Yacht by the king. Added to this figure were 98 miscellaneous vessels consisting of receiving ships, powder hulks, stores hulks, sheer hulks, and also hoys and barges for conveying stores of timber and gunpowder, etc. Receiving ships were obsolete vessels converted to provide temporary accommodation for men entered into the service either as volunteers, sent in as quota men or from impressment before being discharged into the operational ships of the fleet.

Crew Living Locations Within Different Ship Types

Rank	First- and second-rate ships	Third- and fourth-rate ships	Fifth and sixth-rate frigates
Admiral	After end of UGDk	Captain's quarters	Captain's quarters
Captain	After end of Qtr Dk	After end of UGDk	After end of main deck
First Lieutenant	Wardroom – after end MGDk	After end of Qtr Dk	Cabin in gun room
RN Lieutenants	Wardroom – after end MGDk	Wardroom – after end UGDk	Gun room on BDk
Captain RM	Wardroom – after end MGDk	Wardroom – after end UGDk	Gun room on BDk
Lieutenants RM	Wardroom – after end MGDk	Wardroom – after end UGDk	Gun room on BDk
Master	Qtr Dk – port side	Qtr deck – port side	Gun room on BDk
Surgeon	Orlop – port side aft	Orlop – port side aft	Cabin on BDk
Chaplain	Gun room aft of LGDk	Gun room aft of LGDk	Not carried
Gunner	Cabin afore Gun Room	Cabin afore Gun Room	Cabin on BDk
Boatswain	Orlop – port side forward	Orlop – port side forward	Cabin at fore end BDk
Carpenter	Orlop – starboard side forward	Orlop – starb'd side forward	Cabin at fore end BDk
Purser	Orlop – port side aft	Orlop – port side aft	Gun room on BDk
Ship's steward	Orlop – port side aft	Orlop – port side aft	Platform – port side aft
Seamen	Lower gun deck	LGDk – forward	Berthing deck – forward
Marines	Middle gun deck	LGDk – aft	Berthing deck – forward
Midshipmen Snr	Orlop – after cockpit	Orlop – after cockpit	BDk – aft of the seamen
Midshipmen Jnr	Gun room aft end LGDk	Gun room aft end LGDk	BDk – aft of the seamen

Abbreviations:

Dk	–	deck	MGDk	–	middle gun deck
Qtr Dk	–	quarter deck	LGDk	–	lower gun deck
UGDk	–	upper gun deck	BDk	–	berthing deck

Gunnery and Weapons

The primary function of the 575 line of battleships and frigates – often collectively referred to as "cruisers" – that formed the main body of the Georgian naval fleet was to seek out, fight and destroy enemy vessels and support large-scale coastal attacks and landings. Such ships were nothing more than elaborate floating gun platforms that could be despatched to any point of the globe for conflict. Unlike the army, which had to move guns across land of varying terrain, limiting both the size and weight of their ordnance they could use, ships could carry guns of far larger calibre and weight and could deliver far greater and more concentrated firepower.

Standard ships' guns were mounted on carriages made from elm, which had the property of withstanding shock: the many bolts, eyes and ringbolts needed for the ropes could be driven through it without splitting the timber; and, if hit by a round shot, it was less prone to splinter

Details of Standard Carriage Mounted Guns

Size	Length of piece	Weight of piece	Weight of gun and carriage	Diameter of the shot	Average charge	Range: Point blank	Range: Maximum at 6 deg	No. of crew*
42	9 ft 6 ins.	3.25 tons.	3.90 tons.	6.68 ins.	14.0 lbs.	400 yds.	2740 yds.	16
32	10 ft 0 ins.	2.90 tons.	3.47 tons.	6.10 ins.	10.6 lbs.	400 yds.	2640 yds.	14
32	9 ft 6 ins.	2.75 tons.	3.27 tons.	6.10 ins.	10.6 lbs.	400 yds.	2640 yds.	14
24	10 ft. 0 ins.	2.60 tons.	3.09 tons.	5.54 ins.	8.0 lbs.	400 yds.	1980 yds.	12
24	9 ft. 6 ins.	2.47 tons.	2.95 tons.	5.54 ins.	8.0 lbs.	400 yds.	1980 yds.	12
24	9 ft. 0 ins.	2.78 tons.	2.85 tons.	5.54 ins.	8.0 lbs.	400 yds.	1980 yds.	12
18	9 ft. 6 ins.	2.10 tons.	2.52 tons.	5.04 ins.	6.0 lbs.	350 yds.	2110 yds.	10
18	9 ft. 0 ins.	2.00 tons.	2.40 tons.	5.04 ins.	6.0 lbs.	350 yds.	1950 yds.	10
12	9 ft. 0 ins.	1.60 tons.	1.92 tons.	4.40 ins.	4.0 lbs.	375 yds.	1320 yds.	10
12	8 ft. 6 ins.	1.57 tons.	1.89 tons.	4.40 ins.	4.0 lbs.	375 yds.	1320 yds.	10
12	8 ft. 0 ins.	1.46 tons.	1.75 tons.	4.40 ins.	4.0 lbs.	375 yds.	1320 yds.	10
9	7 ft. 6 ins.	1.23 tons.	1.47 tons.	4.00 ins.	3.0 lbs.	330 yds.	1730 yds.	8
9	7 ft. 0 ins.	1.15 tons.	1.37 tons.	4.00 ins.	3.0 lbs.	330 yds.	1730 yds.	8
6	8 ft. 0 ins	1.10 tons.	1.32 tons	3.49 ins.	2.0 lbs.	320 yds.	1555 yds.	4
6	6 ft. 0 ins	0.82 tons.	0.99 tons	3.49 ins.	2.0 lbs.	320 yds.	1555 yds.	4
4	6 ft. 0 ins	0.61 tons.	0.73 tons.	3.05 ins.	1.3 lbs.	310 yds.	1250 yds.	4
4	5 ft. 6 ins.	0.56 tons.	0.67 tons.	3.05 ins.	1.3 lbs.	310 yds.	1250 yds.	4
3	4 ft. 6 ins.	0.36 tons.	0.44 tons.	2.77 ins.	1.0 lb.	300 yds.	1225 yds.	2–3

* If the ship needed to fire guns on both sides, the number of gun's crew was divided by two: i.e. 32-pounder = 7.

Below: "Tom Tack's Ghost" by Isaac Cruickshank, depicting a gun deck, typical seaman, and hammocks overhead. Unfortunately Cruickshank has erroneously shown land pattern gun carriages with iron trucks (wheels), which would not have been fitted, iron being detrimental to wooden decks.

into tiny fragments. At this period the wooden trucks – the wheels on which the carriage ran – were each made of a solid piece of elm sliced from the trunk of the tree. The carriage was built with the minimum amount of material required to support the weight of the iron gun barrel,

whilst ensuring that the resultant recoil forces generated when the gun was fired were directed towards the rear axletree to prevent the gun from overturning. Unrestrained, a 32-pounder gun could recoil some 40 to 50 feet on a flat surface – the width of most ships. To reduce recoil, the guns were restrained by a heavy breeching rope that passed from the breech, or rear of the gun, down through a ring on each side of the carriage and then to the ship's side, where it was secured to two ring-bolts clenched to the hull structure. When the gun recoiled, the forces placed on the breeching rope could exceed 12 tons of pull. Breeching ropes were always three times the length of the gun barrel to ensure that the gun recoiled a sufficient distance to permit reloading. Once reloaded, the gun was then run out by the crew hauling the side tackles, which were rigged between the carriage and the ship's side.

Each gun was equipped with the following items:

I breeching rope	To reduce recoil and take the shock.
I preventer breeching rope	Secondary rope rigged to 24-, 32- and 42-pounders because of their heavy recoil.
2 side tackles	To run the gun forward through the port before firing.
I train tackle	Fitted between rear of carriage and deck at the centreline to move carriage backwards.
I stool bed	Loose fitted on the carriage to support gun breech and quoin.
I quoin (occasionally 2)	Wedge-shaped block laid upon stool bed used to adjust gun elevation.
I pair of wooden handspikes	One set per two guns: levers for raising the gun breech to alter elevation or depression and for moving the carriage sideways or other directions.
I rammer on a stave	To ram home the gunpowder cartridge, shot and wads.
I sponge on stave	To sponge out the gun to remove burning debris after firing.
I wadhook	To remove debris and remains of a cartridge, also to unload the gun on misfire.
I flexible rammer and sponge	Used to load and sponge the gun when the gun port is shut or when fighting at close quarters.
I gunlock	Flintlock mechanism to fire the gun.
I length of slowmatch	Specially prepared rope in salt petre that continuously burned, used for firing the gun if gunlock fails.
I matchtub	Used to contain the slowmatch, the matchtub was filled with sand for safety.
I powder horn	Filled with fine powder for priming the gun and gunlock.
I salt box (I per 2 guns)	Used to contain two ready-to-use cartridge bedded in salt to keep them dry.
I sand scuttle	Ready-to-use sand for putting out fires and sprinkling on the deck to prevent slipping.
Quill firing tubes	Kept in a pouch by the gun captain, they were inserted into the vent to fire the gun, to provide instant ignition.
I cartridge pricker	Kept by the gun captain or his second for piercing the cartridge when loaded.
I vent reamer	Used to clear the vent of carbon deposits that built up after prolonged firing.
I lead apron	Fitted and tied over vent of the gun for safety when not in use – guns were always charged ready for firing.

Carronades

Introduced in 1779, the carronade differed from the conventional type of gun by virtue of having a shorter barrel and being lighter in weight. With exception to its range, this relatively new type of weapon had many advantages over the standard carriage-mounted gun, in that it could deliver a far greater size of shot in proportion to the actual weight of the gun; moreover, the proportion of gunpowder charge was considerably smaller than the weight of the shot. Most carronades were mounted on a slide carriage, which took the brunt of the gun's recoil. The entire carriage was mounted on a fixed block at the front end and transverse casters at the rear, which allowed the gun to be trained far more easily to effect angled firing.

Designed to fire a spherical projectile at a lower velocity over a shorter range than its equivalent long gun, the damage inflicted by the carronade was far greater as the shot did not punch straight though timber but made great splinters. If charged with grape shot or canister shot – i.e. a tin containing 500 musket balls – the carronade proved lethal to personnel at close range. Besides having a greater arc of fire, the other advantage of the carronade was that it required fewer men to operate it.

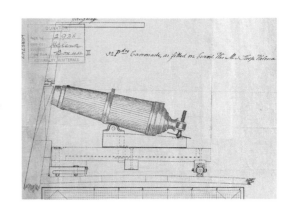

Carronade on a slide carriage showing the fixed block and transverse casters which enabled the gun to be trained. The gun was elevated or depressed by adjusting the screw assembly fitted behind the breech.

Mortars and Howitzers

These weapons were mainly used on bomb vessels, which were employed to bombard coastal installations and fleets of ships as they lay in a sheltered anchorage or harbour. Unlike standard guns, which fired solid-iron shot, mortars and howitzers fired a huge hollow spherical shell of either 10 or 13 inches in diameter charged with up to 11 pounds of gunpowder and a timed fuse. Fired at a high trajectory, these shells could attain a range of just over 4,000 yards. Nearly 4.5 tons in weight, but only 5 feet 3 inches in length, these weapons were mounted on a large turntable-type carriage that could be trained without moving the ship. Because mortars were relatively dangerous, they required much expertise to fire them. By 1803, this task was undertaken by the Royal Marine Artillery. Prior to this date, bomb vessels had to embark Royal Artillerymen, which, as they were land soldiers rather than sea soldiers, presented management problems to the ship's commanding officer when they were on board.

Swivel Guns

Used mainly as an anti-personnel weapon, these guns, which were generally mounted along the bulwarks of the upper decks, fired either a single shot of half a pound or a canister shot of musket balls. Aiming these guns was made easier by having a tiller cast integral with the breech. Usually three feet in length, they weighed about 56 pounds and fired a half-pound ball of one and a half inches in diameter. The standard charge used was about three ounces of powder.

Small Arms

Besides the heavy ordnance, the gunner carried a host of hand weapons used for close-combat fighting. These weapons comprised muskets, bayonets, pistols, pikes, cutlasses and tomahawks.

Muskets

The muskets used in the Georgian navy were of the sea-service type that had a shorter barrel of just 39 inches in length suitable for the confines of a ship. Colloquially called the "Brown Bess", they were formally called "Tower Guns" of the India pattern. Originally manufactured in India under the authority of the East India Company, these weapons were shipped to Britain where they were issued by the Ordnance Board from the Tower of London. When issued, they came in three parts: lock, stock and barrel, the three components then being assembled to fit as one single unit. The term Brown Bess derives from the time when guns were issued from the Tower during the

Typical flintlock pistol used by officers.

reign of Queen Elizabeth I, or "good Queen Bess". The word brown was added to "Bess" because the preservative method used to prevent rusting – a mixture of urine and oak wood shavings – turned the barrel brown. Fired using a flintlock mechanism, these guns fired a ball of just under three-quarters of an inch in diameter a maximum effective range of about 100 yards. Loading was via the muzzle using a metal or wooden ramrod. When not in use, guns were kept in the gunner's storeroom or in chests within the gunroom. In most cases each gun was equipped with a bayonet of about 15 inches in length and a sling, which enabled the weapon to be carried on the shoulder.

Pistols

The gunner also held sea-service pistols, which had a barrel length of 14 inches. Sea-service pistols were distinctive because of their ball-shaped butt covered with a brass cup. When in close quarters, these weapons were often difficult to reload once fired and were often used as clubs. Loaded and fired in the same manner as a musket, pistols had a maximum – though not accurate – range of between 80 and 100 feet. Most sea-service pistols had wooden rammers, to avoid corrosion in a salt atmosphere, and an integral belt hook on one side.

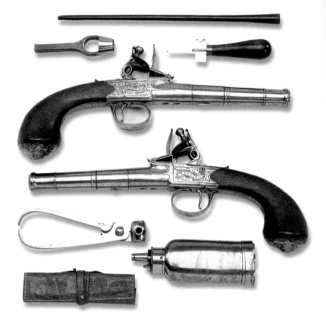

Pair of officers' pistols complete with wooden ram rod, hand-held bullet mould, brass powder flask, and various other accessories.

Pikes

Correctly referred to as "half pikes" to distinguish them from the very long pikes used in land warfare during the 17th century, the shorter pikes used on ships were about seven feet in length. They were made from an ash shaft one and a half inches in diameter, with a three-sided steel point of about four inches in length; points were later four sided. Because the half pike proved highly successful for defending the ship against boarders – at arms length they gave a man a nine-foot reach – these weapons were often referred to as boarding pikes. In larger ships, pikes were placed in racks surrounding the base of the masts where they were readily accessible; otherwise they were kept in the gunner's storeroom.

Cutlasses

By far the most reliable and effective hand weapon of the period, the standard cutlass was simply a steel blade fitted with an iron "double globe" hand guard and grip. Although the seamen were trained in cutlass drill, when it came to battle there was no finesse as the cutlass was simply used as a cut, slash and thrust weapon. Before 1804, the blade was relatively straight with a blood groove on either face, while the hand grip was a plain iron sleeve fitted over the tang of the blade and retained by riveting over the hand guard. A new pattern, formally introduced in 1804, saw a heavier blade with a pronounced curve, and the hand grip, now made in cast iron, was horizontally ribbed for better grip. Like all other weapons, these were kept under the charge of the gunner.

Swords and Dirks

Commissioned officers used swords and dirks. Usually quite ornate, these swords were straight bladed and made of high-quality steel with an elaborate hand guard. Alternatively, the officers used hangers, which had a curved blade similar to those used by cavalry officers. Dirks, more commonly used by the midshipmen, were effectively elaborate daggers.

Tomahawk or Hatchet

Whichever it was called – tomahawk or hatchet – this simple, double-headed weapon comprised an axe measuring about two inches broad and five inches in length with a curved spike 2 inches long at the opposite end of the head. Proving highly effective in close quarters, this weapon was responsible for causing most of the head injuries sustained in hand-to-hand combat.

Above: Officer's hanger (curved sword) with its leather and brass scabbard. Dated 1805, this example is reputed to have been used by an officer at the battle of Trafalgar.

Centre: Midshipman's dirk. This example is unusual in that the blade is much broader than the standard type, which resembled a dagger, used at the period.

Grappling Hooks

In addition to the hand weapons, grappling hooks, with their attached coils of rope, were used to grapple onto another ship and aid men to swing on board. They were made in varying sizes: the larger type – between about 1 foot 6 inches and two feet in length – had four hooks furnished with barbs; the smaller, triple-hooked type was only six inches long. In battle, these were distributed around the upper decks ready for use. They were also slung from the yardarms of the lower yards to catch into the rigging of enemy ships. Other grapnels, furnished with an iron chain instead of rope, were carried for use of towing away fireships.

Other Weapons

Other weapons used were blunderbusses, notable for their bell-shaped muzzle, seven-barrelled volley guns, useful for opening fire on enemy boarders, and boat guns, which had a special mounting to fit into a pedestal to absorb the recoil. These weapons fired either a half- or a one-pound shot. Other weapons kept on board, though little used, were rockets. Pointed knifes or daggers were rarely used as weapons. The reason for this is that the type of knives used by the seamen during the course of their day-to-day duties – rigging and other rope work – had no point to them, but rather a bluff end with one straight cutting edge. The practice of grinding the points off seamen's knives had long been accepted in the navy, simply to avoid murder or injury as a result of quarrels. The design of a seaman's knife today originates from this custom.

Blunderbuss with its typical bell shaped muzzle.

John Cranford of   *Sunderland Durham.*

Campdown
11 Oct 1797

The Sailor who nailed the Flag to   *the Main Top Gallant mast head.*
on board the Venerable, Lord   *Duncan's Ship, after being*
once Shot away by the Dutch Admi.l   *de Winter.*

Drawn by M.r Orme on board for the Express   *purpose of Introducing into his*
Picture of L.d Duncan's Victory now Engraving by   *Subscription & which includes Portraits*
of the Admirals & Officers who so Gloriously   *Distinguished themselves on the*
ever Memorable 11. of October 1797.

Proposals may be had & Subscriptions   *Received by M.r Orme.*

Pub. according to Act of Parliament Nov.r 21.t 1797, by M.r Orme N.o 23   Holles S.t   Cavendish Sq.e & E.Orme 25 Conduit St. Hanover Sq.e London.

Opposite page: "Heaving the Lead" by John Atkinson shows the standard dress of a seaman: white duck trousers, tight-fitting brass-buttoned blue jacket, sennet hat and bright neckerchief.

Right: Seaman John Crawford nailing his ship's colours to the mast at the battle of Camperdown, 11 October 1797. This painting by Daniel Orme epitomizes the tenacity of the British sailor in adversity.

SEAMEN AND MARINES
THEIR TRAINING AND RESPONSIBILITIES

The notion that most men serving on the "lower deck" of a man o' war were conscripts forced into the navy by notorious press gangs is a popular and somewhat misleading concept. Like the officers, the majority of the seamen serving in naval ships were professional men, who came, for the most part, from the English counties that were associated with sea-related trades.

Most men who entered the navy, either as volunteers or through impressment, came from sea-related trades, the mercantile and fishing fleets, or from areas with some connection to the naval dockyards. Unlike the officers, who had influence and advantage, the professional seamen simply needed employment and income, and although pay in the merchant service was higher, the Royal Navy did hold some advantages. Besides the areas of Cornwall, Devonshire, Hampshire and Kent, a good number of seamen came from the dock areas in east London – watermen from Wapping, for example. Besides English, Scots, Irish and Welsh, the navy also included Manxmen and Channel Islanders.

Unlike today's navy, the Georgian navy also embraced men from many different seafaring nations, most of whom, it appears, had served in the mercantile service. Left in a foreign port without a ship, these men had either volunteered or, as was often the case, found themselves pressed into a British man o' war by indifferent naval captains short of crew. In some cases, foreigners, together with British subjects, were taken out of British merchant ships and, although Britain's colonial influence was another contributory factor towards encouraging volunteers, others simply joined for the adventure. Political oppression was another factor that persuaded foreigners to enter into the navy – for instance, there were some 108 Frenchmen (opponents of Napolean) fighting in British ships at the battle of Trafalagar, four of whom were in Nelson's *Victory*. Using the *Victory* as an example, her crew at Trafalgar, excluding Nelson, comprised 820 officers, marines, seamen and landsmen, of whom only 62.6 per cent were Englishmen. Added to this number were a further 22.4 per cent of Irish, Scots and Welsh, while the remaining 15 per cent of the crew were of mixed, foreign or unrecorded origin.

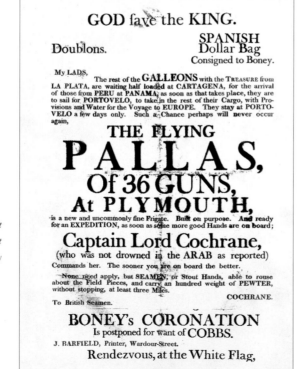

Recruitment poster, the wording of which – "Stout Hands, able to rouse about the Field Pieces, and carry an hundred weight of PEWTER without stopping, at least three Miles" – clearly defines the physical ability required of men being sought by the navy.

Volunteers

Volunteers consisted of both men and boys. As today, men joined for reasons of patriotism or were drawn by the attraction of travel and adventure together with the prospect of a steady wage. One merchant seaman, George Watson, volunteered after simply visiting friends on board the 74-gun ship *Fame* in 1808. Volunteers, as shown in many recruiting posters, would receive a bounty of up to 20 pounds, which for the average labourer was about one year's wages. There were also those who volunteered to avoid the law, and although their intentions appear less noble, enticed by a bounty they avoided prison by paying their debts, irrespective of hardships to follow. The reputation of a ship's captain could also encourage volunteers, especially if he was renowned for capturing prize ships, as a seaman would receive a small share of the ship's monetary value in addition to his earnings.

This illustration shows the press gang in a poor light, for the cartoon manipulates public sympathy by depicting two physically unsuitable victims along with distressed women.

There were also "volunteer boys" who, not to be confused with those entering with intent on becoming an officer, came from the poorer classes. Most, it appears, had either been turned out of or had run away from their homes, and with little prospect of survival without crime, the navy seemed the preferable alternative. Many boys entered into the navy from the Marine Society, set up by Jonas Hanway in 1756 to provide an orphanage for "waifs and strays". After reaching the age of 12 or 13, these lads, provided with a bible and suitable nautical clothing, were sent into the navy as third-class volunteer boys who initially became servants for the lieutenants, earning about four pounds per annum. Conditioned to life at sea from an early age, these boys often became first rate seamen who, in time, formed the backbone of the Royal Navy.

The Impressment Service

Conscription into the Georgian navy came in two forms: impressment and the Quota Acts. The Impressment Service, supported by its tool, the Press Gang, has been portrayed as a deplorable organization and is somewhat over dramatized in contemporary caricatures, popular consensus (influenced by misguided historians), film and television. In truth, impressment was the fundamental instrument that provided the government with the power to call upon its own subjects to defend the sovereign state in wartime – a concept identical to national conscription implemented during World War II. Equally misconceived is the word "Press", the origin of which comes from the French verb *prêter* meaning to lend or to give money in return for service. Re-utilized in the form of exchanging the "King's Shilling" for enlistment into the army, in time the word "prest" became "press", hence "impressments". Because the navy had long used this system, the idea that seafarers could find themselves pressed into the navy during times of war was an accepted one.

The long war with France between 1793 and 1815, however, necessitated a greater demand for manpower. As a result, the press became far more active than on previous occasions, and some used force rather than coercion to assemble sufficient numbers of men. Unfortunately, it is from this, together with contemporary, politically motivated caricatures and popularized images portrayed in today's television programmes and films, that the modern idea of impressment is founded. The wretched man dragged from his trade – or worse, from his new bride, as depicted by less-than-reliable sources – was certainly not what the navy really needed. What the press gangs were actually after were good prime seamen who knew ships and how to live in them, men from the merchant fleet and fishermen – tough men who knew their trade, could knot, splice and hand sails. As a result, the merchant navy and fishing fleets were ripe recruiting ground for the Royal Navy.

The Press Gang Ashore

On shore the Impressment Service generally operated from a "rendezvous" commanded by a lieutenant served by a party of loyal seamen. Naturally most rendezvous were set up in either a commercial, fishing or naval port. One example is the Wrestler's Inn in Great Yarmouth, where James Sharman, later to serve as an ordinary seaman in the *Victory* at Trafalgar, was recruited.

"Liberty of the Subject" by Gillray, illustrating a misfortunate tailor being pressed into service, irrespective of the fact that he appears physically unsuited to survive the rigorous life at sea. Pandering to public sympathy, the group also includes the victim's wife, angry women and distraught children.

Sharman, together with James Secker, a Royal Marine Sergeant, carried Lord Nelson down to the ship's cockpit after the admiral had been fatally shot. In retirement, Sharman became the Keeper of Nelson's Monument that had been erected near the Dene Sands at Great Yarmouth. Charles Dickens would base his character Mr. Peggity on Sharman for his novel *David Copperfield*.

Such was the navy's need for men at this period, it was not unusual to find the Impressment Service setting up such "recruiting stations" in towns further inland. Those that entered the navy from the shore-based press gangs were first taken aboard a receiving ship moored off shore where they were "regulated" before being sent into an active warship in commission. The regulating process evaluated the potential candidate's status – i.e. able seaman or ordinary seaman according to ability, or if inexperienced, he was rated as a landsman – after which he was enrolled to receive pay and, if he was a volunteer, paid his bounty. If the man was married, necessary arrangements could be made to allot pay to his spouse, who would otherwise have had to rely on the parish or on poor relief in his absence.

Besides issuing slop clothing, the regulating process also determined the man's physical condition – it was not uncommon to find that up to 25 per cent of those "pressed in" were immediately discharged as unsuitable for service. Ironically, some of this group, it appears, may already have suffered from scurvy which, though often thought of as being a seaman's disease, was equally common on land, especially when diet was limited during winter.

Not all men could be taken by the Press; certain tradesmen, shipwrights for example, apprentices and persons of particular station held protection papers that legitimately absolved them from impressment. Although this should have guaranteed their liberty, it was not always the case. Shipwrights bringing a newly built vessel into Portsmouth from a private Hampshire shipbuilder's yard were seized by the Press and incarcerated in a receiving hulk – a petition supported by strike action by the private shipwrights eventually brought about their release.

The Press Gang Afloat

It had long been established that captains of ships held the prerogative to make up their crew numbers by their own means, especially when their ships were due to sail. This was resolved in the use of what was colloquially termed a "hot press", which comprised a lieutenant-in-command, petty officers, seamen and marines. Sent on shore by boat, this party of men searched taverns and other haunts for unfortunate victims. Often compelled to use more force than was desirable, it was gangs such as these that gave the Press its historic notoriety.

If insufficient men could be found on land, the sea always proved productive. It was not unusual for captains of undermanned men o' war to target homebound merchant vessels in the English Channel for manpower. Having been ordered to "heave-to in the King's name", naval boarding parties would press the best seamen out of the unfortunate vessel, sometimes leaving little crew remaining to handle the ship they had boarded. Compared to land-based impressment, the Press Gang afloat could always secure prime seamen. Such practices were later fictitiously personified in the play and film *Billy Budd*.

The Quota Men

As the war progressed, it became necessary to supplement the efforts of the Impressment Service by introducing the Quota Acts. Passed under an Act of Parliament by William Pitt the Younger in 1795, this statute obliged each county and city, and even specific large towns, to provide the navy with a predetermined quota of men per annum according to demand. London, for example, had to enlist some 5,700 men, whereas less populated areas, such as Yorkshire, had to provide only one fifth of this figure. Although this system was effectively conscription, bounties had to be

This illustration by James Gillray typifies the stubborn yet jovial countenance of the true British tar.

A TRUE BRITISH TAR.

"Damn all Bond-Street-Sailors I say, a parcel of smell-smocks! they'd sooner creep into a Jordan than face the French! – dam me!"

offered to entice other volunteers. Bounties, which stood at around five pounds in 1793, rose to as much as 70 pounds by the end of the century.

While the Quota Acts did fulfil the numbers required for seamen, quotas for marines fell short of that demanded by law and therefore the whole concept seems to have failed. Besides not fulfilling the expected numbers, the system had other failings. While most magistrates instigated the Act to rid themselves of undesirable community members – poachers, tramps, vagrants, etc. – others took advantage of the legislation

THE INDIGNANT TAR.

to empty their prisons of petty criminals – men who would undermine the social ethics of true seamen. As a result the contents of ship's journals and punishment lists clearly show that there is a direct relationship between the increase of non-seamen conscripts into the service and the rise in both crime and punishment. It was a situation that would not improve as the war progressed.

Others who entered the navy via the judiciary system included people such as debtors, who, taking the bounty to pay for their release from prison, found refuge in the navy. Smugglers, whose criminal activities were not fully regarded as anti-social, were often coerced into the navy as an alternative to prosecution, where their seamanship skills proved an invaluable asset to the service. The navy did not take hardened criminals such as murderers and thieves; such men were either

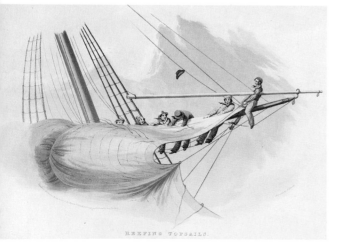

hanged or deported. The Quota System did introduce better educated men into the lower deck but, unlike the common sailor, these men were less tolerant of their lot. Their dissatisfaction led to unrest, disorder and greater insubordination within the fleet and this ultimately led to the mutinies of 1797.

The Rates

Seamen were categorized according to ability and experience. Excluding the Boys Third Class, the seamen essentially comprised three rates: ordinary seaman, able seaman and petty officers; among the latter were the boatswain's mates. These skilled group of men were mainly made up those who worked aloft, handling the sails and their associated ropes, knotting and splicing, operating the rigging and dealing with the anchors, as well as other boat work. Without detailing precise jobs, each would be allocated to one of the ship's two or three watches, and were further divided to work specific tasks at each mast. The younger, most nimble men, known as topmen, precariously worked on the higher yards where agility, combined with dexterity, was essential. The older, sturdier seamen worked on the lower yards, where strength rather than deftness was more vital, while those of long standing and trustworthiness formed the afterguard, working on the quarter deck and mizzen mast. Irrespective of whether they were topmen, afterguard or otherwise, most of these men would be working at the guns in battle. Most seamen earned about one pound and fifteen shillings per month, a wage comparable with that of a common labourer.

"Unloading a Collier" by Atkinson. Note how a bench has been utilized to assist the landsmen hauling on the ropes while the seaman sits astride controlling the load.

Landsmen

This category of men comprised those pressed in or volunteers who had no seamanship skills and were subsequently employed to add weight to hauling ropes, turning capstans, or any other unskilled work where "brute force" was beneficial. Although formal training for these men was not always promoted, the captains of some ships did encourage them to go aloft into the lower rigging to gain confidence. As a result, quite a number of landsmen developed into prime seamen.

Each seaman was issued with two hammocks and bedding comprising a blanket and a bolster, which were supplied through the purser and charged against the man's wages. (Although it is often said that the seamen made their own hammocks, they were usually manufactured by contractors who provided all manner of canvas goods for the navy and military alike.)

The seamen's clothing, commonly known as "slops", was also provided by the purser, who kept official accounts of clothing issued, the costs of which were again deducted from the seamen's wages. Slop clothing was held in a special store situated next to the purser's cabin on the orlop deck. The term "slops" originates from a type of loose shirt called a "sloppe". Although there was no official uniform at this period, the style of clothing issued was standardized and was chosen for its practicality at sea. Most seamen owned the following items:

Trousers	*White, blue or striped, these were made from duck, linen or jean. Ocasionally knee-length breeches were worn.*
Shirts	*Linen or jersey – either plain white, or red or blue chequered pattern.*
Shoes	*Usually black with silver buckles.*
Sea boots	*If worn, these were usually of knee length and made from leather.*
Stockings	*Woollen or silk.*
Headwear	*A tarred sennet (straw) or felt hat, alternatively a Monmouth cap or a Dutch cap with flaps to protect the ears in foul weather.*
Long apron	*Protective garment of coarse linen, felt or leather.*
Belt	*Leather with a sheath for a knife.*
Neckerchief	*Silks of various colours, black becoming common after 1805.*
Short jacket	*Usually blue with brass buttons, sometimes with white braiding over the seams for utilitarian purposes, i.e. to strengthen the seams rather than denoting a mark of rank.*
Foul weather coat	*"Rug" or frieze.*
Waistcoat	*Red, yellow or striped kersey.*

"Jack taking a quid of tobacco for comfort in a storm". The seaman shown is wearing a typical frock to protect his breeches.

After the pay increase in 1797, an able seaman would receive a monthly wage of about 31 shillings and sixpence. This equated with the average pay for a farm labourer. The only extra money he could earn would be prize money received after capturing a ship. Obviously this bonus was much sought after as it would greatly augment his poor wages.

The Marines

All ships of the line, frigates and sloops carried a contingent of marines, whose number made up some 19 per cent of the ship's company. Originally comprising sea-service soldiers made up from various Regiments of Foot, the marines were re-established as Royal Marines by royal proclamation under George III on 29 April 1803. Recruited in the same manner as that used by the army, most marines volunteered for the duration of hostilities. At the beginning of the war with France in 1793, the number of marines in service amounted to just 5,000. By 1802 this figure had risen to 30,000, where it remained until the war with Napoleon ended in 1814. To encourage recruitment, bounties of up to 30 pounds were offered.

The Royal Marines were separated into four divisions: the First Division based at Chatham, the Second Division at Portsmouth, the Third Division at Plymouth and the Fourth Division at Woolwich. Each of these divisional barracks held 40 companies of marines including companies of the Royal Marine Artillery, which would be drafted to operate the mortars on the bomb vessels within the fleet.

As a professional fighting military unit both afloat and ashore, the marines had two duties. Under normal sailing conditions at sea they were generally employed as sentinels guarding the admiral's and officers' quarters, the powder rooms, magazines, the spirit room and other important storerooms. Whilst undertaking these duties they would wear their recognizable uniform of red coat, white pipe-clayed crossbelts, off-white coloured breeches, black leather knee-length gaiters, leather neck band, and black shako-style hat with its distinctive red and white plume. Each man was armed with a loaded musket and bayonet. If not on guard duty, the marines provided general manpower, giving assistance to the seamen where unskilled heavy labour was required – hauling on heavy ropes when the ship was manoeuvring, manning the capstan bars to help turn the capstan when weighing anchor, or carrying heavy loads on board the ship. According to orders, no marine could be officially compelled to work aloft, however some did oblige as volunteers. Some of these, it appears, later became professional seamen at their own will.

During battle the marines provided extra manpower to operate the guns, with most consigned to act as a powdermen who would have been ready to leave their posts to repel boarders. On deck, they formed a disciplined defence at close quarters, providing the necessary small arms fire with their muskets and leading the boarding parties onto other ships. They were also used to form an amphibious assault force for staging attacks on coastal installations and cutting-out (capturing) enemy ships at anchor. Parties of marines were often sent ashore to protect captured storerooms, powder magazines or even prisoners.

In most ships the marines lived and messed separately from the seamen. This preference was a largely unwritten rule for seamen and the marines alike. The marines' quarters on ship depended on the ship type or class. In a three-decked first- or second-rate ship they lived on the middle gun deck, on a two-decked third- or fourth-rate ship at the after end of the lower gun deck, and in the single-decked frigates they lived at the after end of the berthing deck. Each of these locations was in close proximity to the wardroom of the respective ship type. This was of fundamental importance, as the location of the marines' quarters provided a barrier between the officers and seamen in the event of a possible insurrection – a safeguard that proved essential after the mutinies of 1797.

A typical 74-gun ship would have about 120 marines on board as part of the ship's total complement of 550 crew members; the number in a first-rate ship was greater – the *Victory* at Trafalgar, for example, had a company of 146 marine officers and men.

The uniform of a Royal Marine Private comprising a red coat, white breeches, gaiters, and shako with its plume; his leather neck band can just be seen under the dark collar.

A PRIVATE of the ROYAL MARINES.

THE WARRANT OFFICERS
THEIR TRAINING AND RESPONSIBILITIES

Included within the framework of the ship's company were a number of warrant officers: men with specialist skills whose responsibilities and duties ensured the day-to-day running and maintenance of the ship. Unlike the wardroom officers who, when promoted to lieutenant, received their commission from the Admiralty, the status of warrant officer was granted separately by the Navy Board. What divided these men from the common seaman was literacy. According to Admiralty Regulations and Instructions 1808: "No person shall be appointed to any station in which he is to have charge of stores, unless he can read and write, and is sufficiently skilled in arithmetic to keep an account of them correctly." Existing account books, documents and letters from the period clearly support these requirements. Confusingly, this group of officers are subdivided into four categories, the first which held wardroom privileges, the remainder being of "lower-deck" status.

Above: Uniform of a Purser circa 1812. White breeches had been superseded by white trousers, and bicorn hats were now worn "fore and aft".

Opposite page: A typical purser by Rowlandson.

Group Categories of Warrant Officers

1 Wardroom/Gunroom	2 Standing Officers	3 & 4 Petty Officers – Lower deck	
Master	Boatswain	Master-at-Arms	Cook
Surgeon	Gunner	Sailmaker	Caulker
Purser	Carpenter	Armourer	Ropemaker
Chaplain		Carpenter's Mate(s)	Sailmaker's Mate(s)
Schoolmaster			

The Master

As the most senior warrant officer, the master held overall responsibility to the ship's commanding officer for all matters concerning navigation, pilotage and the manner in which the ship was sailed. Because of this all navigational aids, charts, compasses, nautical tables and associated astronomical instruments came under his charge. He would also have been responsible for the rigging, sails, anchors and cables, as well as the ship's "trim" – the way the ship sat evenly in the water – and consequently took responsibility over the stowage of provisions: if they were not loaded correctly, both the ship's sailing abilities and stability would be compromised. His lesser duties covered the security of the ship and the issue of spirits to the crew. The master also held the official ship's journal, or logbook, which, in the event of an incident, loss or grounding of the ship, was provided as evidence at the subsequent court martial. His pay, according to the rating of the ship on which he served, varied from £88. 4s. 0d. to £151. 4s. 0d. per annum. Thus, on the larger ships, his pay was equal to that of the senior lieutenant. Although his seamanship skills were much to be respected, many wardroom officers resented the master's ability to have an "air of consequence" or the "astonishing impudence to think himself your equal".

"Mr Sullivan, Master of the Victory *at Trafalgar" by James Graham. This sketch is wrongly titled, as the Master of the* Victory *at Nelson's famous battle was Thomas Atkinson. However Sullivan may have held this post later.*

While many masters had entered the Royal Navy from the mercantile fleet, others had either side-stepped from midshipmen or lieutenant for a quicker, but limited, promotion, or had worked up from quartermasters and mates of the lower deck. One notable master was William Bligh, who in his earlier career had learned considerable navigation skills from Captain James Cook. Others, we see, later held higher posts. Thomas Atkinson for example, who had been master of the *Elephant* at the Battle of Copenhagen in 1801, and of the *Victory* at Trafalgar in 1805, became master attendant at Halifax Dockyard, Nova Scotia in 1806, second master attendant at Portsmouth Dockyard in 1810 and first master attendant at Portsmouth in 1823.

The Surgeon

Having learned his profession as a civilian, a surgeon would enter the navy after sitting an exam at Surgeon's Hall in London, or alternatively by a Physician of the Fleet if overseas. Once given his warrant by the Navy Board, he would then serve a period as a surgeon's mate before being promoted to surgeon. There were 710 surgeons disposed throughout the fleet between 1793 and 1814. A surgeon's overall responsibilities lay in ensuring the general health of the entire ship's company, attending to their day-to-day injuries and ailments, performing operations, dealing with battle casualties and the management of the ship's sick berth. A surgeon's pay, after 1805, was about £200. 15s. 0d. per annum. While it has often been imagined that the majority of naval surgeons were incompetent drunkards – and it cannot be denied that a minority of them fell into this category – most surgeons had great aptitude. This is evident not only by the fact that most could amputate a limb and close the wound within two minutes, but also by the way in which they kept the overcrowded ships free from contagious disorders and the manner in which they dealt with tropical diseases, using what was effectively homeopathic medicine. What is often forgotten is that naval surgeons spent much of the time at sea miles from any safe or friendly harbour and, as they were so isolated, they were forced to act very much on their own initiative when confronted by a variety of situations.

Caricature by Tegg. Sailors hated being sick as surgeons would stop their rum ration!

The Purser

Although paid the same rate as a boatswain or a gunner, the purser was effectively a civilian provisions manager attached to the ship and responsible for the procurement of all foodstuffs, beer, spirits, clothing, bedding and tobacco. Even though these items were supplied through the naval stores system, the purser had to put up a bond out of his own pocket as security against loss, which was often risky.

As a businessman, he had to ensure that he took his own precautions against financial loss, so it was an accepted practice that he could make a commission of 12.5 per cent per weight of provisions issued. In time this led people to believe that a purser would, for example, fraudulently short measure the crew by issuing 14 rather than the statuary 16 ounces to the pound weight, the difference of one-eighth legitimately accounting for "ordinary wastage". Some pursers would clearly use this to their advantage, but there were many who went bankrupt in an attempt to keep within the legitimate guidelines. One of the grievances petitioned by the seamen in the Great Mutiny of April 1797 was the short measure of victuals. In June that same year, pursers were officially instructed to lay "aside the ancient weights and measures pursuant to public order", which virtually abolished the 14-ounce pound.

Besides issuing hammocks and bedding, for which the seamen paid, the purser also issued slop-clothing, on which he made a commission of five per cent. He also made money on tobacco, to which each man was entitled two pounds weight per lunar month; retailing it at 1s. 7d. per pound his commission was ten per cent. As a purser would receive an average income of only £47. 2s. 0d. per annum, the ten per cent income from the sale of tobacco was quite lucrative. Funded from a special allowance, pursers also procured coal and wood for the galley fire and heating stoves for officers' cabins and the lower deck, lanthorns, candles and moulds for making them, and "turnery"– the wooden eating implements used by the crew.

The Chaplain

As a warrant officer, the naval chaplain of the 18th and early 19th centuries held the same wardroom rank as the master and the surgeon, but, unlike these officers, his position was not essential to the day-to-day running of the ship. As a result, very few were allocated to ships of less than third-rate status. All chaplains entering the navy during this period were clerics of the Anglican Church. Their main duty, which followed the requirements upheld by the Articles of War, was to hold divine service every Sunday for the entire ship's company, irrespective of whether crew members were Roman Catholic, Scottish Presbyterian, etc. Besides attending to routine burials, they also held services of thanksgiving after battle. In many cases, their previous training in theology, the classics and languages often proved advantageous, enabled them not only to bring spiritual and social relief during long periods at sea, but equipping them also to translate intercepted foreign despatches. One chaplain noted for his linguistic skills was Reverend Alexander John Scott, who, after being ordained in 1792, entered the navy the following year as chaplain of the *Berwick*. In 1795, he was invited by Admiral Sir Hyde Parker to become both chaplain of his flagship and his private secretary. Six years later, and still with Parker, his language skills were used to assist Nelson when he was arranging the Convention of Copenhagen. In 1803, he became Nelson's chaplain and confidential secretary, a role in which he examined all French, Spanish and Italian letters, newspapers and captured despatches. He would even go on shore in disguise to gather intelligence.

Pay for naval chaplains was relatively low and, although this was given a marked increase to about £12. 10s. 0d. per month in 1812, the wage had always been supplemented by an allowance of one "groat" or fourpence for every crew member listed on the ship's books. His extra income, therefore, depended on his "parish", which in a first-rate ship with a complement of 850 could be £14. 3s. 0d. Although chaplains "messed" in the wardroom, in ships of the line they were generally berthed in a cabin within the gun room, situated at the after end of the lower gun deck. Apart from the antiquated pay system, little has changed in the 21st century: the naval chaplain still enjoys the benefits of the wardroom, albeit on larger ships such as aircraft carriers and destroyers. The only marked difference between the chaplaincies of Georgian times and today is that the modern fleet now also has Roman Catholic priests and Presbyterian ministers to accommodate other denominations.

The Schoolmaster

Usually only carried in line-of-battle ships, the primary task of the schoolmaster was to teach the midshipmen mathematics, trigonometry and theoretical navigation. Before being accepted into the navy, candidates for the position of schoolmaster were examined by representatives of Trinity House at Deptford Strond to prove their ability to perform these duties. The emphasis, naturally, was placed on navigation. Besides teaching potential officers, schoolmasters were also encouraged, according to Admiralty Regulations and Instructions, to teach "other youths of the ship ... whether reading, writing or otherwise". Having no specific status, most schoolmasters messed with the midshipmen and found their own place to berth, although in some ships a schoolmaster may have been lucky enough to have been given a cabin, as was the case with the chaplain within the gun room.

The Boatswain

The boatswain was responsible to both the ship's master and its captain for all aspects of rigging, sails, blocks, general cordage, anchors and cables, ship's boats and all other matters of seamanship. Besides being highly skilled and experienced in his trade, he was also ranked as one of the ship's standing officers, who remained with the ship, working as a "ship-keeper", while the vessel was laid up in "ordinary". The practice of retaining certain ship-keepers maintained continuity, especially with regard to a particular ship's rigging equipment – information that was invaluable to a new commanding officer or master when a ship was re-commissioned. Besides undertaking daily inspections of the rigging, the boatswain ensured that his mates, his petty officer assistants, turned the watches of seamen out on deck to attend to sail-handling duties and other necessary ship operations.

As a standing officer, he had his own cabin within the ship near the location of his expansive storeroom. Holding a vast quantity of stores, equipment and sails under his charge, he presented monthly accounts to the captain of the items bought or expended during the course of his duties.

Right: Boatswain circa 1820 with his pipe (whistle). Though of later date, beards being unfashionable during the Georgian period, the clothing shown is typical, especially the red waistcoat.

Portrait of John Adams by Cruickshank. Adams served as a Boatswain's mate under Nelson in the Agamemnon. He is shown dressed in his formal attire as a Greenwich Pensioner in later life.

To avoid fraudulent practices, his stores were periodically mustered and inspected by boatswains from other ships and, likewise, he would be called upon to administer the same service elsewhere. One of his main responsibilities was to ensure that all sails were in good repair, aired and well dried before storing for, if left damp, there was a chance that they could catch fire by spontaneous combustion. Should the ship be docked for a refit or careened, the boatswain had to ensure that all his stores were removed from the ship and transferred to a secure "lay apart" store designated within the dockyard. When any work had been completed, he was responsible for mustering his equipment and re-embarking it onto the ship. His other duties, as indicated within the Captain's Orders of the frigate *Amazon* in 1799, were to ensure that, when at anchor, the external sides of the ship from stem to stern were "washed, swept and cleared of loose yarns, oakum and every kind of dirt from the gunwale down to the waters edge; and upon all occasions to watch that no clothes lines or ropes whatever are hanging or towing over the chains, gunwales or head".

Despite the fact that they were mature in years and highly experienced in the execution of their duties, it appears that boatswains characteristically got into trouble from time to time through drunkenness, and it has to be said that theft of stores was also not unusual.

In 1808, a boatswain's annual pay amounted to about £57. 12s. 0d. if he was serving on a first-rate ship, while the minimum wage was £36. 12s. 0d.

The Gunner

Equal in seniority to the boatswain, the gunner, as a warrant officer, held full accountability to the ship's captain for all the ship's ordnance – the magazines, gunpowder, shot, cartridges, gunlocks and any other gunnery associated equipment, such as rockets, small arms and hand weapons. Unlike the majority of the ship's company and officers, who were removed from the ship when it was de-commissioned, the gunner, as a "standing officer" remained with the ship when it was laid up in ordinary. This is verified by the length of service of William Rivers, gunner of the *Victory*. Rivers was attached to the ship from 1793 to 1811, during which time the ship was put in ordinary from 1797 to 1800, rebuilt between 1801 and 1803, and further laid up for repairs between 1806 and 1808.

Working in unison with Inspector of Ordnance from the Ordnance Board, the gunner inspected all guns and their carriages embarked onto the ship, as well as all associated stores supplied from the Ordnance Board. Before embarking gunpowder, he had to ensure that all magazines were dry and fit to receive it. Besides gunnery equipment and stores, he was also responsible for overseeing the gunner's mates, quarter gunners, yeoman of the powderoom, gun captains, and the training of all the gun's crews.

Because the gunner held a vast quantity of stores and equipment he, like the boatswain, would have to present monthly accounts to the captain of the items consumed in the course of his duties. He would also have to provide accounts showing the quantity of powder, shot or musket ball expended through gunnery and small arms training. As was the case with the boatswain, the gunner was subject to having his stores periodically inspected by other gunners to check for fraud, and gave similar service when called upon to do so. Should the ship be docked for a refit or to be careened, he had to ensure that all his stores and guns were removed from the ship and temporarily stored within the dockyard. After the work had been completed, he would then have to muster his equipment and re-embark it onto the ship. Unlike the other two standing officers, the gunner did not have a cabin in the true sense, but berthed in a partitioned area in the gunroom at the after end of the lower gun deck in two-decked ships and above, and messed with the gunner's mates and the junior midshipmen.

He would have started his career as a seaman and, having showed aptitude as a gun captain, would have risen to gunner's mate. He would spend considerable time at sea training all the guns crews to fire "at a mark". Although for the most part self-taught men, close examination of existing personal papers of one gunner, William Rivers, clearly show that he had a good knowledge of both mathematics and trigonometry and a fine grasp of ballistics and chemistry, as well as good practical experience in explosives and projectiles. These papers also indicate that this knowledge was further expanded by receiving periodical training at the Royal Arsenal at Woolwich, where new theories based on recent experimentation and invention were taught. Generally "rough" in nature, by virtue of their lower-deck background, on the whole gunners were

Sea-service pistol with belt hook. Operated with a flintlock mechanism, the weapon is 19 inches long, with a barrel length of 14 inches. The brass cupped butt proved useful when the weapon was used as a club after firing.

steady, reliable characters and were much respected by the officers and crew alike. His annual pay, equal to that of the boatswain, was about £57. 12s. 0d. if serving in a first-rate ship, or £36. 12s. 0d. in a sixth-rate ship.

The Carpenter

As the third standing officer, the carpenter differed from the boatswain and gunner inasmuch that he would have served a seven-year apprenticeship learning his entire profession on shore and would, therefore, originally have come from a civilian background. In most cases, he would have then spent at least a further seven years working at his trade (as either a carpenter or a shipwright) before entering the navy. To be appointed carpenter on a ship he must have at least "served an apprenticeship to a shipwright, and [have] been six calendar months a carpenter's mate of one or more of His Majesty's ships". It appears that quite a number of these men had actually worked within the Royal or private dockyards or been impressed from merchant ships.

Like the boatswain and gunner, the carpenter had to hold a vast quantity of stores and equipment and presented his monthly accounts of the items consumed in the course of his duties to the ship's captain. His storeroom was always located near the boatswain's store at the fore end of the orlop. Besides his own specialist range of tools, his stores comprised a vast assortment of nails, bolts, copper and lead sheathing, paint, door locks, glass, glue, tar and pitch. He also kept considerable quantities of timber for hull repairs and spare spars, the latter of which was pre-prepared timber roughed down to size ready for replacing specific yards or topmasts made to measure for his particular ship's mast specifications. One of the many tasks we find the carpenter attending to was fitting "fishes", a form of splint, to masts that had sprung (cracked) during severe weather conditions. As with the other two standing officers, the carpenter's stores were regularly inspected by other carpenters to check for evidence of deception. Unlike the main body of the ship's crew, the carpenter did not keep watches. Because of this, carpenters, as day workers, were often termed "idlers".

Besides undertaking general repairs, the carpenter's daily duty was to sound the level within the ship's well at regular intervals to determine whether water had leaked into the hold and to get it pumped overboard. He was responsible for the entire maintenance of the pumps, for if they failed, both the watertight integrity of the ship and its safety could be disastrously compromised. In addition, accumulated bilge water could have a detrimental effect on the health of the crew. To assist him, he had a carpenter's crew, the number of which varied according the size of ship. When the ship went into battle, the carpenter and his crew stationed themselves in the lower regions of the ship where, armed with wads of oakum, nails, sheet lead and wooden bungs, they worked to plug shot holes below the water line. This particular responsibility, which had first been officially authorized during the reign of Queen Elizabeth I, is not dissimilar to that performed by the damage control parties employed on modern warships. When the ship was docked for a refit or careened, the carpenter would ensure that the hull was well supported with timber shores, and if receiving new masts, each mast would be securely stepped and wedged at all deck levels. While he received the same pay as the boatswain and gunner of fourth-rate ships and below, his monthly earnings were £1 more in larger ships, thereby giving him an annual wage of £69. 18s. 0d.

The Armourer

Working with the gunner was the armourer, whose title, which speaks for itself, originated from his earlier-time duty of care for body armour and weapons. By this period, however, the armourer's main responsibility was to look after small arms; muskets, pistols, cutlasses, pikes, etc. and to undertake all work that related to both a blacksmith and a "fitter". As well as making repairs to iron components throughout the ship, he could also manufacture hinges, nails and bolts, and undertake other forged work, such as repairing gunlocks, padlocks and door locks. Very much the ship's "ordnance artificer" and "engine room artificer" of the modern navy, he may well have acquired such skills in previous employment as a watchmaker, locksmith or "smithy".

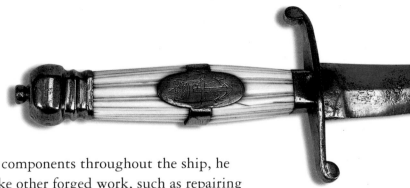

Ornate hilt of a standard Midshipman's dirk.

The Ship's Cook

Stylized by Rowlandson's well-known caricature of a man missing either one leg or one eye, or often both, the ship's cook in reality was not always so physically impaired. Ship cooks were very

often pensioners recruited from Greenwich Hospital who returned to sea in order to supplement their allowances. What is certain is that most were by no means men of great culinary aptitude. As the most junior of warrant officers, the major reason the ship's cook was given such status was because he was in charge of looking after the one major fire hazard on board the ship – the galley stove. Irrespective of his ability to cook, it was his responsibility to ensure that the galley was run efficiently and that the ovens and boiling coppers were thoroughly cleaned for inspection at 3 p.m. each day. This work would be undertaken by assistants selected from the crew who were very likely to be landsmen.

Left: "Ship's Cook" by Rowlandson. Unfortunately this much-used caricature has wrongly suggested that every ship's cook serving in the Georgian navy had a wooden leg, which was not the case!

THE COMMISSIONED OFFICERS
THEIR TRAINING AND RESPONSIBILITIES

From where were most naval officers enlisted? In 1800 the majority, it appears, were from the English counties of Devonshire, Hampshire and Kent, the former being the source from where the highest number came. This appears quite natural, for not only did these counties contain the seats of influential families, but each of these sea-counties had its own related naval dockyard: Plymouth, Portsmouth and Chatham, respectively.

Opposite page: "Master and Commander" by Dominic Serres. This image shows the officer wearing a tricorn (three-cornered) hat, which had, by 1795, been superseded by the more fashionable bicorn (two-cornered) hat worn "athwart" the head.

Below: "Woolwich Dockyard" by Nicholas Pocock.

The second highest areas of origin of officers were London, Cornwall, Norfolk, Somerset and Suffolk: London had dockyards at Deptford and Woolwich and the remainder, of course, are sea-counties. The third group of counties, again bordering the sea, comprised Dorset, Northumberland and Yorkshire. While naval officers were drawn from other counties, their numbers represented less than 0.5 per cent of the naval population. Most surprisingly, Essex and Sussex, which both have coastal boundaries, come into this lower category. Generally Scottish officers came from the east coast counties of Aberdeenshire, Fife, Lanarkshire and Midlothian, primarily because these areas supported coastal and fishing trades. Most officers entering the "King's Service" from Ireland originated from the counties of Cork, Dublin, Tipperary, Westmeath and Wexford, which, besides being the most populated, are all sea-counties. Wales, because of its low population, yielded the least officers – in this case most came from the sea-counties of Carmarthen, Glamorgan and Pembrokeshire.

Beyond the British Isles, the majority of officers entering the service came from North America and the West Indies, the numbers from each being roughly equal. In North America, most Canadian officers originated from Nova Scotia with its naval bases of Halifax and St. John. With regard to the recently formed United States of America, one has to remember that all those born in these once-British colonies were, before the Declaration of Independence on 4 July 1777, strictly subjects of the British monarch and were consequently expected to fight for Britain. Of this group most came from Massachusetts, New Hampshire, New Jersey, New York, Rhode Island and Virginia. Those entering from the West Indies mainly came from Antigua, which had a naval dockyard, Barbados, Dominica, Nevis and St. Kitts. As for Europe, the main sources were Hanover, Gibraltar and, quite surprisingly, France. In the latter case, these men would have been Royalist emigrants escaping revolutionary tyranny.

Social Background

In terms of their social background, naval officers came from five distinctive social groups: (1) peers or baronets; (2) landed gentry; (3) professional men; (4) commercial businessmen; and (5) working class. Of the first group, peers, which comprised 12 per cent, most were sons of peers, who, due to their inevitable involvement within the House of Lords or because they had to operate their estates, would often be officially absent from duty. As a result, while 45 per cent of peers did achieve post rank, only 45 per cent made flag rank. Officers titled baronets, unless titled through inheritance, would have attained this status by virtue of their distinguished service within the navy. Indeed, many that conferred the title of baronet had actually originated from professional families – admirals such as Collingwood, Jervis, Nelson, Pellew and Strachan, for example, as well as captains such as Ball, Blackwood and Hoste, to name but a few. Unlike the peers, most of these men had already attained flag rank.

The second group, landed gentry, which made up 27.5 per cent of the officer class, faired poorly – only 30 per cent attained post rank and a mere 20 per cent achieved flag rank. By far the greatest number of officers came from families of professional standing, who can be categorized, with approximate percentages, in the following order: (1) Naval – 48; (2) Church – 17.5; (3) Military – 15; (4) Law – six; (5) Civil Service – six; (6) Medicine – five; and (7) Ministers,

"Mr Blockhead promoted to Lieutenant" by George Cruickshank highlights the fact that some officers attained their commissions by virtue of social status rather than ability.

diplomats etc. – two; (8) Miscellaneous arts etc. – 0.5. Having either a father or an uncle within the service (the first source) certainly influenced young men to follow the same profession, especially when their relative could use their influence to ensure patronage for easier promotion.

The second source comprised families of ecclesiastical connections such as university theologians and those with rural parishes. Nelson, for example, Britain's foremost naval hero, is typical of this group: his father, the Reverend Edmund Nelson, served as the Rector of Burham Thorpe, a remote village in of Norfolk. Nelson, incidentally, also had family connections to the navy through his mother: his uncle, Captain Maurice Suckling, later Comptroller of the Navy, secured the young Horatio's first patronage on his 64-gun ship *Raisonnable* in 1771. While some 41 per cent of this group became post captains, only 6.5 per cent reached full admiral status.

Category three centres around those with a military background. While one son of these influential families would invariably seek a clerical career and another joined the army, it was inevitable that the other would join the navy. Interestingly, the percentages reaching post or full flag rank from this category are virtually parallel to those that came from a church-based family. Parents in the Civil Service, often in strategic government or admiralty positions, would often use their influence to seek opportunities for their sons. Irrespective of this, few officers entering with such advantages made higher ranks beyond post captain. The reasonably high percentage covering those originating from the medical profession is somewhat encouraging, especially when physicians and doctors were, at that time, considered relatively low-placed on the social scale, and few of this profession, it must be remembered, were either wealthy or had influence.

The fourth significant source of officers were business- and commercial-based families – those connected with ship building, ship owners, in various trades and even tenant farmers, the key factor being wealth, which could open many doors. While 54 per cent of this group did not make post rank or higher, it is of equal note that some 18 per cent of the category did make flag rank.

The final group of naval officers came from the working class, where neither money nor privilege could influence their advancement. Naval or merchant seamen by profession, these men, though less privileged, had raised themselves from what is colloquially termed the "lower deck" through personal endeavour and recognized qualities. Commencing their careers as ordinary or able seaman and elevating to either master's mates or master, it was generally those of the latter two ranks that made the transition to commissioned officer. Few officers entering from influential backgrounds could surpass the proficient abilities of these lower-deck men. However, in the long term, experience and accumulated knowledge was not enough for further promotion: of this group only 13.5 per cent reached post captain and a mere 2.5 per cent made flag rank. Of the remaining 84 per cent, most of these men never achieved rank beyond lieutenant, mainly because of age. The other reason why promotion was limited was the patronage system encouraged by senior officers of the influential classes looking out for their own kind. Despite the system's inherent faults, some lower-deck officers did achieve distinction – more as a result of their seamanship and navigation capabilities than through honour in battle. Examples of such are James Cook and William Bligh, both of whom had been ship's masters with exceptional navigation skills.

Cook, a Yorkshireman from near Whitby, first came to prominence after charting the St. Lawrence river for the attack on Quebec in 1759. Sponsored by the Royal Society, Cook, given command of the *Endeavour*, then undertook voyages of discovery into the Pacific Ocean, charting Polynesia, Australia and New Zealand. On his third expedition, in 1779, Cook was unfortunately killed by angered natives at Karakakooa Bay, Hawaii. Bligh, a Cornishman brought up in Plymouth, served for four years as master of Cook's ship *Resolution* during that fatal voyage in 1779. However, he is better known for commanding the ill-fated *Bounty* and for its infamous mutiny in 1789, when he was cast adrift along with 18 others in an open boat and sailed 3,600 miles, losing only one man. After successfully undertaking a second breadfruit expedition, he later fought with exemplary distinction, commanding the 74-gun *Director* at the Battle of Camperdown in 1797 and the 64-gun *Glatton* at Nelson's Battle of Copenhagen in 1801, where, after the battle he "was sent for by Lord Nelson to receive his thanks publicly on the quarterdeck". After taking up the post of Governor in New South Wales in 1806, Bligh returned to Britain in 1811 where he was promoted rear admiral of the Blue, but he never went to sea again: he died of cancer in December 1817, aged 63.

While there are many other examples of officers entering from the lower deck, two others who were well known were John Pasco and John Quilliam, both lieutenants serving on Nelson's *Victory* at Trafalgar. Pasco had initially joined the 28-gun *Pegasus* as a boy in 1784, before serving as a gunner's servant. It was another 11 years before he became a lieutenant. Serving as first lieutenant in the *Victory* in 1805, Pasco held promotional seniority over his fellow officers. However just before battle commenced, he was demoted to signal officer. His senior position was given over to John Quilliam, *Victory*'s sixth lieutenant, so that the junior officer might gain a promotional advantage that would not otherwise have been readily open to him. Two months later, Quilliam was directly promoted captain. A Manxman by birth, Quilliam had entered the navy as a pressed man, reaching the rank of lieutenant in 1798. Although promoted over Pasco, he never attained flag, dying of natural causes in 1829. As for Pasco, he was eventually promoted in 1810, despite

Opposite page: "Lord Nelson" by Simon de Koster, 1801.

losing the use of his right arm, and, after commanding *Victory* much later, was elevated to flag
rank in 1847. He died in 1853.

Entering and Advancement

Potential officers entered the service by one of two methods: indirectly through the Royal Naval
College at Portsmouth or directly by voluntary enlistment onto ships as "servants".

Naval colleges

Opening in 1729, the Naval College provided formal training and education to those candidates
from the peerage, baronetcy and landed-gentry backgrounds. Annual intake comprised some 40
boys aged between 13 and 16. Subject matters covered in training included mathematics, physics,
astronomy, gunnery, fortifications and theoretical seamanship. However, while attempts were
being made to formalize officer education, the most common question, "What is the use of book
learning for sea officers?", remained.

Many senior officers, preferring the alternative and well-accepted method where captains chose
potential candidates themselves, regarded the Academy as "a sink of vice and abomination". This
judgment carried an element of truth, as many of the Academy's pupils resorted to drink and
gambling rather than take lessons. By 1800, the demand for new officers had increased; with
numbers at the college swelling to about 90 per year. As a result, training began to improve and
by 1806 the college's buildings were expanded. By the late 18th century, a second college, the
Naval Academy, had opened in Gosport; this took similar numbers of candidates to the Naval
College in Portsmouth.

Volunteers

Irrespective of the existence of the two naval academies, the long-tested system of volunteers being
enlisted directly onto a ship as "captain's servants" remained the standard practice until 1794.
While this method placed the responsibility for officer selection entirely in the hands of a ship's
captain, the system was often open to abuse. For example, it was customary for captains to enlist
their own sons, nephews, or sons of their close friends. It was not uncommon for some captains,
encouraged by promotional or political self interest, to take youngsters from well-connected
families on board, youngsters who were quite unsuited to meet the standards expected to make a
good sea officer. Whether good or bad, the system did create an established social clique, and that
benefited the requirements of the navy at the time.

In many cases, the names of these youngsters were carried on the ship's books well before they
were eligible, or physically old enough, to go to sea. This was termed "early entry". From the
perspective of the protégé involved, the main advantage in such a practice lay in accumulating the
necessary number of years required to count towards future advancement. However, as the child
concerned was too young by law to draw wages, his pay went direct to the captain. Receiving pay
for a boy who was not even on the ship could be conceived as morally inappropriate, but providing
that the protégé listed was a real person, this practice was deemed legitimately acceptable.
However, if a captain was found to have entered false names into the ship's books in order to draw

pay for himself, by law he was guilty as charged. Because the state paid the wages, and was therefore party to the contract between the ship's commander and his protégé, the servant's position was not dissimilar to that of an apprentice. Nelson was himself entered into the navy under these means: his uncle, Maurice Suckling, enrolled him into the ship's books at the age of 12, even though Nelson did not join the ship until March 1771.

A captain was entitled to four servants for every 100 people carried in the ship's books; if the captain was knighted, his entitlement was doubled. Servant posts were also granted to lieutenants and masters; the system therefore made allowance for sons or nephews of men from these ranks to enter the service. The choice of selection, however, lay exclusively with the ship's captain.

This system of selection – often referred to as "old entry" – was superseded, under the Admiralty Order-in-Council of 16 April 1794, by what was classified as "volunteer entries". While this effectively abolished the concept of officer's servants, captains, lieutenants and masters were financially compensated for the loss according to their servant number entitlement: The actual wording of the Order-in-Council read: "And no Boys should be allowed to be borne on the books of H.M. ships in future under the denomination of Servants to the Captain, Lieutenants and Warrant Officers: but instead thereof a certain number to be borne on separate list after the Ship's Company, in classes of the following descriptions."

The new system provided three categories of volunteers: Classes I, II, and III. Officer recruits belonged with Class I, which, according to the Order, was "to consist of young gentlemen intended for sea-service … to be styled volunteers and allowed wages of £6 per annum". This non-servile group not only comprised sons, nephews and protégés of other officers and gentry entering after 1794, but also included those previously enlisted as captain's servants. Within 50 years, those within this group became known as Naval Cadets. Those entering as Class II or III Volunteers, which relate to the lower deck, have been discussed earlier .

Career Advancement
(*in descending order*)

	Rear admiral of the Blue
Admiral of the Fleet	Commodore of the Red
Admiral of the Red	Commodore of the White
Vice admiral of the Red (after 1805)	Commodore of the Blue
Rear admiral of the Red	Post Captain
Admiral of the White	Commander or Master & Commander
Vice admiral of the White	First Lieutenant
Rear admiral of the White	Lieutenant
Admiral of the Blue	Midshipman
Vice admiral of the Blue	First Class Boy or Volunteer Servant

The inevitable goal of potential officers was to attain flag rank of admiral but, as with any profession, it meant enduring years of service as well as good fortune. While the first is easily understood, the latter – luck – needs some explanation. Service in the Royal Navy, especially during war, was a rigorous occupation involving long periods at sea where deprivation, disease, a monotonous and unbalanced diet, risk of injury, life or limb, capture by the enemy, or even a lapse in discipline, could all take their toll on the likelihood of career advancement. In effect, reaching a high rank was down to chance and the odds were heavily stacked against you, especially during times of war.

Midshipmen

Whether they were captains' servants, first-class volunteers or candidates from a Naval Academy, each of these "young gentlemen" aspired to become a commissioned officer. Although the majority were aged between 14 and 18, the promotion of petty officers from the lower deck meant that the age of midshipmen could range from between 12 to 40. It was not unusual to find some midshipmen (who had entered the service via selection in their teens) nearing 40 years of age having continuously failed their exams.

Midshipmen above the age of 14, often called "oldsters", held an equivalent rank to a petty officer, while those of lesser age, referred to as "youngsters", were usually rated as able seamen; Nelson himself held an able seaman's rate while in the 28-gun *Seahorse*. This hierarchical difference formed a natural demarcation: the oldsters berthed and messed in the cable tier or after cockpit on the orlop, whilst the youngsters berthed separately in the gun room on the lower gun deck above, under the watchful eye of the gunner. This division made sense, for when the older midshipmen had wives or women on board, the most junior members of the crew would certainly not have been welcome. Equally, in the interests of the welfare of his protégés, this arrangement also best suited the captain. When at sea, it was quite natural for the youngsters to congregate with their elders, but, regardless of whether some may have been berthed on the orlop, they remained juniors by the standards of the cockpit. Such unwritten rules led to a ceremony termed "the fork", where, at 8.p.m. when the first watch of the night commenced, the midshipman acting as president of their

"The Midshipman's Berth" by George Humphrey. Dated circa 1821, this image captures the cramped conditions and boisterous spirit of the "young gentlemen".

mess drove a fork into a beam. This simple act indicated when all youngsters were to clear out of the mess and go back to the gun room or their hammocks. Those who were allowed to stay, having achieved equality with their compatriots, would no doubt have considered themselves significantly advanced.

Also sharing the midshipmen's mess, by virtue of their mixed status, were the schoolmaster, assistant surgeon and the captain's clerk. With exception to the captain's clerk, who had his own cabin on the orlop, the former generally berthed in the gun room on the lower gun deck. As befitting the natural personalities of teenage men, the atmosphere within the midshipmen's mess, although very civil, was often highly boisterous; more often than not the schoolmasters and clerks would have joined in the revelry. The midshipmen's berth also had its fair share of social problems – bullying and corruption were not uncommon .

Having proved their ability to perform their duties, midshipmen received a certificate of qualification from the captain and pay equal to that of an able seaman.

At sea, midshipmen generally worked ship in a three-watch system. The senior of each watch was stationed on the quarter deck, the second on the forecastle and the third abaft the mizzen mast; the remaining, less-experienced, midshipmen worked under them, their numbers varying according to the ship's size. Often serving as master's mates, their duties comprised recording soundings, marking up the log slate, and bringing all matters to the attention of the officer of the watch. At noon, using either quadrants or sextants, they would take observations to determine the ship's position, and, having recorded their findings, noted them down in their own journals, which were inspected by the captain. Other duties involved taking charge of signalling and

Above: "The Progress of Midshipman Blockhead" by George Cruickshank. The perilous rock standing in the path of the boat is symbolic of the career upon which Blockhead has set his course.

commanding the boats. When working aloft, one midshipman would be stationed in each mast top, maintaining communication with the deck whilst ensuring that his men, furling and reefing sails, worked efficiently and in silence.

One midshipman was allotted to each of the ship's divisions. His duties involved ensuring that the seamen within his division had both sufficient and clean clothing, that men who were ill reported on the sick list and that hammocks belonging to his men were brought up and stowed. When preparing for battle, he would make sure that all gunnery equipment and powder cartridges were at hand and that all the guns under his charge were ready for action. When in harbour, according to the Captain's Orders for the *Pegasus*, three midshipmen were to man the upper deck during daylight hours and two at night.

Between keeping watch at sea, midshipmen spent most of their time studying mathematics, navigation, trigonometry and seamanship: the former three subjects were taught by a schoolmaster, if one was carried within the ship. The remaining time was spent writing up journals. By the age of 19, following some six years' service, a midshipman was ready to take his examination for lieutenant. The system, however, was not entirely rigid, and some midshipmen took their exams at an earlier age.

The examining board, comprising three senior captains, convened for the most part on the first Wednesday of every month. After reading the candidate's journals and certificates of service, the three officers would proceed to question him on general seamanship, including his watch duties under sail and practical items such as splicing rope and reefing sails. He was assessed on aspects of navigation: shaping courses, determining a ship's progress and position by dead reckoning and calculation, sun and lunar observations and calculating compass variation and understanding tides; matters of discipline were also considered.

Unfortunately, this exam was often little more than a formality – indeed, it was not uncommon to find that one or more of the examiners was the father, a relative, or a friend of the young man's family. Although this irresponsible practice did prevail, Admiral Middleton, Lord Barham, formalized the exam by ensuring that it contained specific questions. Once the candidate had passed the exam, he was promoted to the rank of lieutenant (if there was a vacancy), and received his status of "commissioned officer" from the Admiralty. As a result, he was moved from the cockpit to the wardroom to join his fellow officers.

Lieutenants

The number of lieutenants within a ship varied according to the type of vessel: first-rate ships carried eight; third-rates, five; fifth-rates, three; sixth-rates, two, and one in the larger sloops. Experienced lieutenants were given command of vessels such as small sloops, armed cutters, gun brigs and armed schooners: Lieutenant Lapenotoire, who commanded the schooner *Pickle* which brought home news of the Battle of Trafalgar, was one such officer. Another notable seaman who captained a ship holding the rank of lieutenant was William Bligh, who commanded the *Bounty* in 1789. In retrospect, Bligh should have been promoted to commander in recognition of undertaking such an expedition. The standard pay for a lieutenant at this period amounted to about £100. 16s. 0d. per annum.

A lieutenant's duties, according to Admiralty Regulations, were to execute all orders directed by his captain or senior lieutenants with "punctuality and diligence". Taking command on deck as the officer of the watch at sea, his main concern was to ensure that the ship maintained its correct course and bearing, and to be on the alert to prevent rigging and sails from becoming damaged by sudden changes in wind strength or direction. He was also responsible for making sure that the midshipmen, mates and seamen under his command were "alert and attentive to their duty". If faced with any problems, unusual occurrences, or a sudden change in weather, he was to call the captain on deck immediately.

Excluding the smaller ships, which had one or maybe two lieutenants, each ship had a first lieutenant, who, being senior by virtue of experience and ready for promotion, was directly accountable to the captain for the administration of both the ship and its crew. His responsibilities encompassed a wide range of management matters, such as implementing watch and quarter bills, which listed where all officers, seaman and marines were stationed when on watch or in battle. This same list also designated individual tasks to each man to cover any given situation: sail handling, manning pumps, fire fighting and boarding parties, to name but a few. A lieutenant was also responsible for the day-to-day running of the ship – allocating where the men were berthed, maintaining the cleanliness of the ship and, equally important, maintaining discipline amongst the crew. In most cases the first lieutenant did not keep watches, but would be obliged to be on deck for any reason determined by the officer of the watch. In battle, the first lieutenant stood with the captain on the quarter deck, and if the captain should fall, the first lieutenant instantly assumed command of the ship.

Each lieutenant took command of one gun deck during the battle and was responsible for the firing control of all guns. Aided by midshipmen and quarter gunners, the lieutenant would ensure that all guns had a constant supply of powder and shot and that the men manning the guns remained steady while under fire from the enemy. Those lieutenants not appointed to a specific gun deck either took command of the guns on the forecastle or quarter deck, or were appointed as the communications officer, stationed on the poop deck to oversee signalling.

The first lieutenant and the other lieutenants messed in the wardroom, located at the after end of the deck above the lower gun deck in two- and three-decked ships. In the frigate classes, they lived within the gun room, positioned aft on the berthing deck. While most of the lieutenants may have shared a cabin, the first lieutenant always had his own. If stationed on a two- or three-decked ship, the first lieutenant enjoyed the privilege of having his own private "head" (toilet) within the starboard quarter gallery adjacent to his cabin; the remaining lieutenants would have to share the head located in the gallery opposite. Each lieutenant had charge over one of the ship's divisions and, with the assistance of midshipmen, was responsible for the general welfare of the seamen within his division.

Promotion

Lieutenants could attain promotion to captain or commander by one or more of several paths: (1) patronage from influential superiors; (2) recommendation from his captain; or (3) distinction and conduct in battle. Patronage was generally gained through family, political or naval connections – sons of peers or land owners, for example. This did not necessarily mean that they were good sea officers – some indeed were quite ineffective.

Lieutenants recommended for promotion solely on their ability generally waited on a list of seniority until receiving their appointment from the Commissioners of the Admiralty. Under certain circumstances this rigid, but fair, system could be overruled. Approved by the Admiralty, a Commander-in-Chief of a fleet on foreign service could appoint a lieutenant to either acting-captain or commander, in order to fill a post created by either a death or a court martial. Typical of 18th century naval custom, favouritism was often directed towards lieutenants serving on flagships and because of this many lieutenants eagerly sought to serve on such ships. As advantageous as this opportunity may seem, it was not always the case, for when an admiral shifted his flag to another ship, he often took his captain and chosen officers with him, leaving less favoured ones behind.

Capt. Huxley Sandon.

The third prospect of advancement, distinction in battle, did not always merit immediate promotion, and while it was not unusual to promote the first lieutenant of each ship after a major action, the battle and its result had to be significantly important to warrant such a practice. History shows that some lieutenants may have attained an acting captaincy rank by this means, but they may have been forced to wait a further three to four years to become a full post captain. Nelson was promoted in all these ways in the course of his career. By nature highly proficient in seamanship skills, he was promoted to lieutenant at the age of 18; irrespective of his abilities, his rise to captain at the age of 21 was influenced by his uncle, then Comptroller of the Navy. Promotion could also result from being placed in command of a captured vessel and taking it into the nearest friendly port. Although only temporary, this post certainly proved a lieutenant's ability to command.

Right: "Captain Huxley Sandon" by Rowlandson.

Opposite page: "Captain of Marines" by Rowlandson.

Master and Commander

Often confusing, the joint title of Master and Commander had been introduced in the late 17th century in order to provide an established rank for officers given command of vessels below the sixth-rate status; i.e. sloops and brigs. When it was first introduced, the role of command in small ships was divided between two distinct tasks: that of the master and that of a commander, the latter being effectively a captain. By the end of the 18th century it had became common to carry a master in the smaller ships – therefore in 1794 the rank "master and commander" became obsolete and was replaced by that of commander. However, there was no significant difference between the duties and responsibilities held by these officers and that of a captain – the only real difference lay in the size of the ship, the number of guns on board and the crew. As commanders, these officers were entitled to their own personal cabin, which varied in size and quality according to the spaciousness of the vessel. Restricted in experience and also by a lack of patronage, many commanders found themselves "on the beach with half pay", after holding one, or if lucky two, commissions within a ship. Some 15 years after the end of the Napoleonic Wars, the role of commander superseded the position of first lieutenant as second-in-command on most ships to accommodate this rank.

Captains

Ships of the sixth-rate classes and above were always commanded by a full captain, or more precisely, a post captain, the term "post" distinguishing the rank from the commander who captained the smaller-classed vessels. Most full captains would have held the rank of commander beforehand, but those who had showed distinction only held the position briefly before gaining promotion to post rank. One example is Captain John Bazely, who, holding the rank of lieutenant, commanded the 12-gun armed cutter *Alert* during her successful capture of the American brig *Lexington* in 1777. Rewarded for this, Bazely was promoted to Commander, but because he still had command of the *Alert*, the cutter was consequently up-rated to sloop to comply with his new rank and pay rate. Promoted to captain in 1778, Bazely took command of the 90-gun *Formidable*, Admiral Palliser's flagship, in 1778, this new command being very different from the *Alert*.

Pay for a captain was directly related to the size of the vessel and its crew under his command, hence the concept of rating ships that was introduced during the 17th century. The income for a captain of a third-rate ship, approximately £390. 8s 0d. per annum, was virtually twice as much as that earned by a captain of a sixth-rate ship. Because of this wide variation, many captains competed for command of higher-rated vessels, especially first-rate ships, which carried an admiral and the added benefit of potential promotion to flag rank. Answerable only to his superior squadron commander – a commodore or an admiral – a captain held total supremacy on his own ship.

The captain's personal quarters within a two- or three-decked ship was generally located at the aftermost end of the quarter deck under the poop. Divided into a day cabin, a dining cabin and a bed place, his accommodation was spacious and quite luxurious. In addition, the two quarter galleries either side of the day cabin gave provision for toilet facilities. On first-rate ships a captain had further advantages, for if sailing as a "private ship" – i.e. not carrying a flag officer – then a captain could transfer into the more luxurious admiral's quarters, giving over his own cabins under the poop to the first lieutenant. Captain's of frigates had similar but slightly less spacious quarters located at the after end of the main or gun deck. However, if the frigate was carrying a commodore or an admiral, the captain had to vacate his quarters to his superior and transfer into the first lieutenant's cabin in the gun room. One example of this concerns the 32-gun *Amphion* in 1803, then under the command of Captain Thomas Masterman Hardy. When the *Amphion* sailed from Portsmouth

"Boardroom of the Admiralty" by Rowlandson.

carrying Lord Nelson to the Mediterranean to join the *Victory*, the ship had effectively become a flagship and Hardy would have had to give his quarters over to his admiral. Conversely, when the *Victory* sailed for England as a "private ship" after the Battle of Trafalgar in 1805, Hardy, then in command of that ship, could have used Nelson's quarters. However, as the admiral's quarters contained the body of Nelson, Hardy declined to use his prerogative.

When a captain was promoted to flag rank, he did so by virtue of his seniority above his fellow peers listed in the same system. The notion of having to serve one's time meant that many years could pass before a captain received promotion. The alternative path, commonly referred to as "fortunes of war", potentially accelerated many an officer's advancement. It is, therefore, small wonder why one common toast, "To a bloody war and quick promotion", was hailed by officers in many a ship's wardroom at the time.

Commodore

In the true sense, the rank of commodore was an intermediary post given to senior captains taking temporary command of a small squadron or a shore post of prominent significance. Unlike a captain, a commodore was granted the privilege of flying a pendant at his appropriate masthead, its colour and position reflecting that of the senior admiral to which his squadron was attached. The rank of commodore arose from the need to deploy part of a fleet under the command of one senior captain on a particular assignment, with his temporary "flag rank" giving him overall authority over captains commanding the other ships in the squadron, irrespective of their own seniority – somebody had to be responsible, especially if the assignment should fail.

Typical duties comprised commanding an inshore squadron or a small group of ships, mainly frigates, detached from the main fleet to watch over an enemy port under blockade. Alternatively his duty may have involved making a specific attack. One such case was when Nelson, holding the rank of commodore attached to Admiral Sir John Jervis' fleet, was sent with a detachment of ships to attack Santa Cruz, Tenerife in July 1797; the entire attack failed disastrously, and Nelson lost his right arm in the assault. Another example, although in a different war, saw Commodore Sir

Peter Parker's ineffective attack on Fort Moultrie, Charleston, South Carolina in June 1776. Other typical duties involved commanding squadrons escorting large convoys of East Indiamen, transports and other merchant shipping. This mundane but essential duty was not dissimilar to that undertaken by the Royal Navy during World War II. The appointment of commodore was often only a temporary posting, after which the captain would revert to his own rank and uniform. The more fortunate, however, retained their status until promoted to rear admiral.

Admirals

The hierarchical system adopted for admirals comprised three divisions, each of which contained three ranks. After the Dutch Wars of the 17th century, the entire naval fleet was subdivided into three squadrons, each of which was denoted by a single colour – in order of seniority: red, white and blue – shown on the flag flown at the ensign staff on each ship [1]. The concept of having three coloured divisions originated from the need to mobilize ship groups in battle, in much the same manner as military units were mobilized on the field. Considering that Cromwell's parliamentary navy was commanded by military generals "at sea", this is quite understandable. The three-division system remained in practice until 1864, after which the Royal Navy used the White Ensign only; the Red Ensign was adopted by the mercantile fleets and the Blue Ensign for the Naval Reserve and Auxiliary Services.

Admirals were subdivided into three individual ranks which, in order of seniority, comprised admiral, vice admiral and rear admiral. The origins of these titles were also adopted from the military concept of operating large fleets during the Dutch Wars. The admiral, who had overall command, was generally stationed at the centre of his fleet; the vice admiral – second in command – controlled the van (head) of the fleet, while the rear admiral – subordinate to the other two – supported the rear. Irrespective of the fact that the strategy of warfare had changed at the beginning of the 18th century, the three titles, if somewhat redundant, remained.

Having been promoted from captain or commodore to Rear Admiral of the Blue; i.e. the lowest rank of the lowest squadron, the aspiring officer had to rise nine ranks to attain the senior post of Admiral of the Red. When the rank of Admiral of the Red was repositioned between Admiral of the Fleet and Admiral of the White in 1805, an aspiring officer would then have had to make ten steps. With the abolition of the red and blue ensigns in 1864, the respective titles appending an admiral's rank – red, white and blue – were likewise discontinued.

Gentleman's dressing cabinet commonly used by officers. This functional item of campaign furniture, also used on land, comprised a wash stand and mirror, writing desk, drawers for personal effects, and, at the bottom, a porcelain toilet bowl, with a lead-lined bidet to the left.

Note: 1 The White Ensign was later modified to carry the red St George's Cross to ensure distinction of English ships from those flying the white Bourbon battle flag of the French Navy. The French later adopted the Tricolour circa 1795.

Admiral of the Fleet

The pinnacle of naval authority, the admiral of the fleet had the individual privilege of flying the Union flag at the head of the main mast. Unfortunately those holding this prestigious rank rarely held it long before death removed them.

The Admiralty

Presiding over the Admiralty Board and answerable to the monarch and government was the First Lord of the Admiralty, who could be either an Admiral of the Fleet or a civilian with high political connections. The rest of the board comprised six members, half eminent admirals, the remainder civilians of equal distinction. Although the board members were august in years, they governed the entire organization judiciously and controlled naval policy, its ships and the promotion of officers. They also held political power over the Navy Board, a joint naval and civilian organization that dealt with the financial resources of the navy – ship building, repair and the procurement of naval stores. The Admiralty also oversaw other equally related organizations: the Victualling Board, Ordnance Board, Transport Board and the Sick and Hurt Board, each of which presented their own problems. As the political wing of the navy, the Admiralty Board resided at the Admiralty Office located in Whitehall, adjacent to what is now Horse Guards' Parade. Excluding board officers, the staff within the building numbered about 60, comprising many clerks, administrators and messengers. Most important were the First Secretary to the Admiralty and his second, both highly competent administrators holding considerable authority. Throughout the French Revolutionary and Napoleonic Wars these posts were filled by Evan Nepean and John Croker. Because navigational charts were important, the Admiralty also employed a hydrographer, the post being held during this period by Alexander Dalrymple.

"Admiral Lord Howe on the deck of Queen Charlotte *at the Battle of the Glorious First of June 1794" by Mather Brown. The painting shows various naval and marine officers' uniforms, including that of the admiral. A midshipman can be seen far right.*

LIFE AT SEA
DUTIES, DAILY ROUTINES AND BATTLE STATIONS

It is unrealistically romantic to think that life at sea was packed full of adventure, battle with the enemy, constant danger and hardship. On the contrary, for most of the time life was an endless cycle of keeping watches, manoeuvring the ship, handling sails with monotonous regularity and undertaking remedial maintenance to combat damage sustained by weather and strain.

Naval warships spent less than two per cent of their time actually engaged in battle; the rest of the time was spent watching over an enemy port, seeking out the enemy, preparing the ship ready for either situation, or merely keeping the vessel seaworthy. To run the ship efficiently, the crew were divided into two watches, named to each side of the ship: larboard and starboard. Nordic in their origin, these two names date back to medieval times, before the innovation of the rudder, when ships were steered by a single oar called a "steerboard" fitted to the right-hand side of the vessel when looking towards the prow. When taking on cargo it was necessary to bring the left-hand side of the vessel alongside the wharf or jetty to avoid damage to the "steerboard", hence the left side was termed as the "ladenboard" – the side on which the vessel was "laden" or loaded. In time, the two words ladenboard and steerboard became abbreviated to larboard and starboard and today the former term has been superseded by the word "port", to avoid confusion between larboard and starboard when giving orders in stormy weather. Although the change from larboard to port was not formally introduced by Admiralty Order until 1849, existing logbooks show that some naval officers were unofficially using the word port during time of Nelson.

The Divisions

The larboard and starboard watch of seamen worked alternate shifts and were further divided into teams representing different "parts of ship", at which each man was allocated a dedicated station where he would undertake different tasks. These duties were laid down within the ship's watch and Station Bill, a formal ship's routine and an allocation of manpower drawn up by the ship's captain and master. The men were grouped to work each mast or particular deck areas of the ship: the divisions within a typical ship consisted of foretopmen, forecastlemen, maintopmen and mizzentopmen, waisters and the afterguard. For welfare reasons, each division was overseen by a specified officer and a midshipman.

"Seaman Furling a Topsail" by W. Kohler. In reality, stowing sails was far more physically demanding than the image portrays; likewise, it is unlikely that seamen wore hats aloft for fear of loss.

The topmen were the youngest and fittest of able seamen who manned the uppermost yards on each mast. Robert Wilson, a common seaman, wrote at the time that a topman: "Not only requires alertness but courage, to ascend in a manner sky high when stormy winds do blow; in short they must exert themselves briskly. The youngest of the topmen generally go highest." Captain Marryat, who referred to topmen as "the smartest able seamen" recommended that a 36-gun frigate should have 20 foretopmen and 26 maintopmen, two of whom were to be petty officers or able seamen; the others, training landsmen. In charge of each group was a captain, who was an experienced petty officer. In sailing ships today the captains of these divisions are referred to as the watch leaders.

The forecastle men, overseen by the captain of the forecastle – usually a boatswain's mate – were generally the best, but oldest, seamen in the ship. Being heavier in build with age, these men worked mainly with the anchor gear, which required particular skill; they also operated the sails on the bowsprit. The waisters, stationed in the centre of the ship (i.e. the ship's waist), mainly comprised landsmen who, with lesser seamanship skills, added weight and power for hauling up or bracing round the yards of the fore and main mast. This division also provided manpower for hoisting out the ship's boats, which were housed on skid beams crossing the ship's waist. In time most landsmen became competent seamen, the youngest working aloft, the others working elsewhere as required. The remaining division, referred to as the afterguard, mainly worked on the quarter deck hauling on braces and halliards as required, but they rarely went aloft unless they were required to assist in furling the main sail. These men also worked the setting of the mizzen sail, often referred to as the "spanker", which is the large fore and aft sail set on a boom and gaff yard on the mizzen mast. Certain men from this division may also have assisted with signal halliards.

"Weighing Anchor" by Kohler. This task required upwards of 140 men to man the capstan.

The Daily Routine at Sea

Each day at sea commenced at 12 p.m., when astronomical sightings were taken to determine the ship's position. It was from this time that the daily routine was divided into a seven watch system, not to be confused with the larboard and starboard divisions of seamen. Each watch and its time span was as follows:

Time period (standard time)	Time period (24-hour time)	Watch title	Origins of title
12 noon to 4 p.m.	12.00 to 16.00	Afternoon	Self explanatory
4 p.m. to 6 p.m.	16.00 to 18.00	First Dog	Associated with dog star, Sirius
6 p.m. to 8 p.m.	18.00 to 20.00	Second Dog	As above
8 p.m. to 12 midnight	20.00 to 00.00	First	The first watch of the night
12 a.m. to 4 a.m.	00.00 to 04.00	Middle	The middle of the night
4 p.m. to 8 p.m.	04.00 to 08.00	Morning	Self explanatory
8 a.m. to 12 noon	08.00 to 12.00	Forenoon	Self explanatory

Notes:

1. The reason why two dog watches were created out of one four-hour period was to ensure that the routine altered daily, otherwise the men of each watch would keep the same hours indefinitely.

2. The origin of the term dog watch is uncertain, but it may correspond to the rising of the dog star, Sirius. Alternatively it may relate to laying low, or "dogo", for half the standard watch hours.

3. In the Royal Navy the Second Dog watch was later renamed Last Dog, the title Second Dog being retained only in the merchant service.

Watch	Time	24 hour time	No. of rings
Afternoon	**12.00 noon**	**12.00**	**8 bells**
	12.30 p.m.	12.30	1 bell
	1.00 p.m.	13.00	2 bells
	1.30 p.m.	13.30	3 bells
	2.00 p.m.	14.00	4 bells
	2.30 p.m.	14.30	5 bells
	3.00 p.m.	15.00	6 bells
	3.30 p.m.	15.30	7 bells
First Dog	**4.00 p.m.**	**16.00**	**8 bells**
	4.30 p.m.	16.30	1 bell
	5.00 p.m.	17.00	2 bells
	5.30 p.m.	17.30	3 bells
Second (or Last) Dog	**6.00 p.m.**	**18.00**	**8 bells**
	6.30 p.m.	18.30	1 bell
	7.00 p.m.	19.00	2 bells
	7.30 p.m.	19.30	3 bells
First	**8.00 p.m.**	**20.00**	**8 bells**
	8.30 p.m.	20.30	1 bell
	9.00 p.m.	21.00	2 bells
	9.30 p.m.	21.30	3 bells
	10.00 p.m.	22.00	4 bells
	10.30 p.m.	22.30	5 bells
	11.00 p.m.	23.00	6 bells
	11.30 p.m.	23.30	7 bells
Middle	**12.00 a.m.**	**00.59**	**8 bells**
etc	etc.	etc.	etc.

Commencing at noon, the ship's day would follow this routine:

Time	Bells	Standard Events
12 noon	8	Set the afternoon watch.
		With the exception of a minority of people on watch, the entire ship's company are "piped to dinner" and receive first issue of grog.
		Noon sighting taken to determine ship position.
1.30 p.m.	3	Those on watch who have not yet had dinner are relieved in order to eat.
		Ship's company off watch given time for leisure unless urgent work requires some to turn to working parts of ship or; training at gunnery, small arms or cutlass drill as ordered by the commanding officer. Idlers return to their daily work.
2 p.m.	4	Officers to dinner (this may be as late as 2.30 pm).
4 p.m.	8	Set the first dog watch.
		Hands not on watch to supper and second issue of grog.
6 p.m.	8	Set the second (or last) dog watch.
		Hands from first dog watch not yet having eaten go to supper.
		Officers take supper.
8 p.m.	8	Set the first watch of the night.
		Pipe down – the entire ship's company collect their hammocks from the splinter nettings surrounding the upper decks, take them down below and hang them from the beams ready for sleep.
		On-watch seamen go to the watch station.
		Off-watch seamen turn-in to sleep.
		Lights out – Master at Arms and his corporals douse all lanthorns throughout the ship for safety and to prevent the enemy from seeing the ship at night.
		Officer of the Watch reduces sail to ease work in darkness should the weather deteriorate.
		Lookouts posted on the forecastle, poop decks and either side of the ship, each of which are relieved after one hour.
12 midnight	8	Set the middle watch of the night.
		On-watch seamen roused from their hammocks and called on deck.
		Off-watch seamen go below and turn-in.
		Lookouts posted on the forecastle, poop decks and either side of the ship, each of which are relieved after one hour.
4 a.m.	8	Set the morning watch.
		On-watch seamen roused from their hammocks and called on deck.
		Off-watch seamen go below and turn-in.
		Lookouts posted on the forecastle, poop decks and either side of the ship, each of which are relieved after one hour.
		Officer of the Watch may make more sail, weather permitting.
5 a.m.	2	Cook roused to prepare the galley fires.
5.30 a.m.	3	Ships company off watch roused and turn-to, swabbing upper decks throughout ship.
7.30 a.m.	7	Up hammocks is piped, the entire ship's company take down their hammocks. Once rolled and lashed, they take them up to their appropriate places and stow them in the splinter nettings around the upper decks of the ship.
		Officers and idlers called.
8 a.m.	8	Ship's company piped to breakfast.
		Set the forenoon watch.
		Officer of the Watch makes more sail according to instructions.
8.30. a.m.	1	Idlers commence their daily work.
		All hands not on watch undertake training at gunnery, small arms or cutlass drill as ordered by the commanding officer.
		Alternatively, all hands turn-to and work their parts of ship or are employed as thought fit.
		Mess cooks collect food daily rations from ship's steward.
11 a.m.	6	Officers and ship's company mustered by divisions to witness punishment if required.
12 noon	8	Set the afternoon watch. Ship's company "piped to dinner" etc.

Watch and Quarter Bill listing showing seamen's names against specific tasks.

Ship's time was notified by striking the ship's bell mounted in its belfry at the after end of the forecastle. Time was measured using an hour and a half-hour sand glass; the timekeeper manning the bell rang it every half-hour, the number of rings denoting the actual time. The table on page 76 shows how the bell was rung for the afternoon, dog and first watches. Eight bells were rung to terminate each watch.

With some exceptions for specific tasks, most of the work given to the seamen during the daytime appears quite mundane – taking down or setting up masts, getting guns and stores in or out of the ship, etc. Many accounts endlessly quote "the people employed occasionally" or "the people employed making junk". The former statement does not fully identify what tasks were actually undertaken, but "employed occasionally" implies that the ship's company worked in their various parts of the ship assisting the sailmaker, making new ropes or "mucking out" the livestock if they were carried on board. Others would be occupied sweeping or scrubbing the gun decks. One group, under the charge of the captain of the head, would clean the toilet facilities. Paintwork also needed attention, likewise tar needed to be scraped from the decks after the caulker and his gang had finished their work. As for "making junk", this hapless occupation involved chopping up old rope using a "junk" axe and converting it for other uses – wads for the guns, for example, or teasing out the strands and fibres and mixing them with oakum for caulking the decks. Much of the bi-product produced from junking would, in all probability, have been used to make the 18th century equivalent of toilet paper, in the form of a teased-out pad. This makes good sense, for the tar content within the rope pad had similar properties to the pine extract used in disinfectant today, and recent evidence suggests that oakum alleviates the problem of piles. Other work, evidenced from existing logbooks, would have entailed "picking the bread", which meant removing bread that was unfit for consumption.

When ships returned to their home port for refit, the seamen spent much of their time de-storing the ship, heaving out the shingle ballast and removing the iron ballast before going into dock. They would also have had to de-rig the ship, taking down masts, as well as removing the guns and their carriages.

Apart from the day-to-day maintenance, a ship at sea needed constant attention. Therefore all hands would have been called to bracing stations when the ship was tacking or wearing, or indeed when any other manoeuvre was required. This also applied when making more sail, shortening sail, or when the sails needed to be reefed. This was a time-consuming activity: men could be called to hand or reef sails as often as six times in 14 hours throughout a night. The sails would often get "blown out" in squally winds and therefore needed to be changed. It was during such poor weather conditions that the British seamen demonstrated their true mettle – unbending a torn sail from its yard, sending it down on deck, sending up, bending and setting a replacement sail could all be achieved within nine minutes. Reefing topsails in one frigate took just one and a half minutes.

Weighing the anchor. Besides showing men manning the capstan, this diagram illustrates the anchor cable being nipped to the messenger cable, nippers being removed, and the many seamen down in the cable tier stowing the wet heavy cable.

Seaman catting the anchor by hooking the cat block to the anchor ring. The anchor was then hung vertically from the cathead (large timber bracket) before fishing the anchor to stow it for sea.

Weighing, or coming to anchor, also required the attention of the majority of the ship's company. When weighing anchor, capstans had to be manned by as many as 260 people in a first-rate ship. In addition, there would be some 40 men in the cable tier coiling the great cable down and another 100 people involved with associated tasks. While this was going on, the rest of the crew would be setting sail. Before coming to anchor, the ship's company would haul up the anchor cable from the cable tier where it was stowed and flake it out along the entire length of the gun deck ready for it to run freely out through the hawse hole when the anchor was let go. An anchor cable in a third-rate ship measuring 24 inches in circumference and 101 fathoms in length, would weigh just under 5.5 tons.

Unexpected extreme weather conditions presented a constant threat to ships at sea, or even in harbour and, according to good seamanship practice, measures were taken to avoid either loss or damage to the ship and to ensure the safety of the crew. In squally weather or approaching storms, prudent captains would strike (lower) their topgallant masts and yards. This precaution, which would have involved large numbers of the ship's company manning ropes, would be undertaken to avoid damage to masts and rigging and to remove top-weight, effectively reducing the motion of the ship and subsequent stress on the rigging. In most cases, topgallant yards and masts were lowered to the deck and topsail yards lowered. In extreme conditions, topsail yards were sent down and their respective topmasts were lowered down to the cap of the mast below. Masts could be lowered and raised within half an hour and, while this may appear incredible from our viewpoint today, in Nelson's time such actions would save a ship. These precautions assumed vital importance in the West Indies on Monday 31 August 1772 when a hurricane struck English Harbour, Antigua. Recording the events in his log, Thomas Pasley, captain of the 28-gun *Seahorse*, explains:

"A great swell in the Harbour and the Clouds Contending for different passages in the air at 1/2 past 11 small Breezes began at NNE and incresd gradually untill 1/2 past 5 when it became Violent. began then to be afraid of a Hurricane. am Starbd. Bow fast broke above ? Onbd the Chatham carried away her main yard and and Starbd. Lower quarter Gallery Sprung our Bowsprit and laid the Mizen Channell flatt [sic] to the side at 6 the anchors of

our moorings started together with a Rock to which a Cable of 15 Inches was clinchd let go our Best and small Br. [Bower] Anchors to prevent driving on Berkeley Fort Rocks or out of the Harbour every fast now parted and our anchors Dredging grounded on the outmost point of the new Wharf at 7 the Chatham cut away her Foremast at do. cut the lanyards of our Fore Shrouds and about four inches into the Mast The Falcon at this time thwart our Hause [sic]. But the violence seeming to abate reard wounding our Foremast any further at 1/2 past 8 the wind suddenly reard and became Calm when we discovered the Active on Shore in the bitt between Berkeley Fort and the admirals house with her mast standing but without her Rudder During this interval we Endeavoured to get alongside the new wharf carried Hawser out for there purpose but about 9 and too early for us not having accomplish our wirk [sic] began blowing if possible with double Violence from the South: she never failing Custom of those Horrid Gusts called Hurricanes the hawser Snapd and our Anchors too the Northd. of us in a moment were washed to the opposite shore and laid aground near the admirals House with the Chatham — on our Larbd. Bow and notwithstanding so near the middle of the Day it was impossible to discern the nearest object at 10 Cut away the Foremast and soon after (while we were cutting the Lanyards) the Main and mizzen blew away the ship Righted immediately Laying along before with her Muzzles of the guns in the water although by no means light being victualled and stor'd for three months. The fall of the Main Mast broke the Main yard and Topmast stove the Barge and Rendered the spare Main Topmast and Topsail yard on the Booms unserviceable at 11 began to moderate and Clear Saw the Falcon on shore Dismasted on the Adm.ls. Mastd. Bow as likewise the Active in the same Distress about _ Cable Length to the SW of her being blown from her former… [word illegible]."

"Dismasted Man o' War" by D. Tandy. The artist has shown the ship driven onto a lee shore, flying her ensign inverted to signal she is in distress.

"Captain Sir Edward Berry" by John Singleton Copley. Captain Berry was the commander of Nelson's Vanguard *at the Battle of the Nile.*

In February 1780, extremely squally wind conditions caused the *Albemarle*, later commanded by Nelson, to lose her main topgallant and topmast, part of the main top and her mizzen topmast. This event occurred while sailing between the islands of Nevis and St. Eustatia. Bad weather conditions such as these were not just confined to the West Indies but were also to be experienced in the Mediterranean, as Nelson and Captain Edward Berry, commander of the 74-gun *Vanguard* were later to find in the Gulf of Lyons in May 1798. In a letter sent to his father-in-law, Captain Berry wrote:

"At half-past two the mizen-topmast went over the side; the fore-mast gave an alarming crack, and at a quarter past three went by the board with a tremendous crash, and...it fell in two pieces across the forecastle. Our situation was really alarming: the wreck of the fore-topmast and foremast hanging over the side, and beating against the Ship's bottom; the best bower-anchor was flung out of its place...; the wreck of the main-topmast swinging violently against the main rigging, every roll endangering the loss of the mainmast... Fortunately there was a small rag of the sprit-sail left, and... we got her on the other tack. The bowsprit did not go, though it was sprung in three different places ... We cut the anchor from the bows, and got clear of the wreck, with the loss of a boat and top-sail yard, &c., ...The gale did not abate in the smallest degree, and the main rigging ...was no support to the mast; we struck the main yard, which eased it greatly, and secured the rigging ... We shipped so much water, that it was necessary to scuttle [cut holes] the lower deck, [to drain water lower into the ship to maintain stability] ... Here I have to lament the loss of ... a Midshipman of the name of Meek....For want of masts we rolled dreadfully. The storm did not abate till Tuesday afternoon, which enabled the Alexander to take us in tow. Our situation on Tuesday night was the most alarming I ever experienced; we stood in for the Island of Sardinia, and approached the SW. side of the Island, intending to go into Oristan Bay, ... we ordered the Alexander to cast of the hawser, and desire to shift for herself – trust to our own fate, ...Indeed the Vanguard was a perfect wreck, but the Alexander still had us in tow. Fortunately, at about six o'clock on Wednesday, the 23 May, a breeze sprang up, the Alexander's sails filled, ...and before 12 we anchored in six fathoms..."

Although shipwreck was the worst possible calamity, collisions occured with greater regularity. When Nelson was preparing the *Albemarle* to sail from the Downs with a convoy on 26 January 1782, he wrote in his log:

"At 8 (a.m.) came on a most violent Squall from the Nd. [northward] in the height of which the Brilliant an East India Storeship drove a Thwart our hawse and carried away our Bow Sprit, Foremast Head, ... [illegible] of the Buntlines, Mizen Gaff, Spanker Boom Larboard Cat head and Quarter Gallery together with the Fore, Fore top sail and Top Gallant yards all of which were broke in Sundry places and went over board with the mast, the Wreck we cut away ... nor was we able to save any of the Sails or any part of the Rigging..., the Sheet Anchor was likewise tore away the Stock broke and about 20 fms [fathoms] of the Cable ... it is to be observed that the Ship [Albemarle] is so Crank that before the Brilliant drove on board us our Carpenter was standing by with Axes to Cut away the Main mast, Fearing she might oversett ...

"HMS Dido *and* Lowestoft *in action with* Minerve *and* Artemise, *24 June 1798".*

Struck the main top mast and got down the Top Gallant masts Do. Struck the Mizin[sic] top mast & Cross Jack Yard."

The *Victory*, Lord Nelson's flagship at Trafalgar, also had her fair share of collisions: when arriving at Gibraltar on 1 December 1796: "the Blanche fell on board us and carried away our Fore Yard in the slings". Laying off Cadiz on 3 April 1797, the *Victory* was involved in a second collision when she "ran foul of HMS. Goliath and Carried away our Qtr [quarter] Gallery, Poop Lanthorns and Stove the Cutter". A third collision occurred on Sunday 16 April 1797, the log stating: "Performed Divine Service During which Time the Theseus came on Board us and carried away part of the Larboard Quarter Gallery." No doubt this event cut short the chaplain's sermon.

The Men and Ships in Battle

The primary purpose of the man o' war and its crew was to seek out and give battle to the enemy. To achieve this, the entire ship's company was constantly trained at gun drill, cutlass drill and small arms fire. Each man had his dedicated place of duty, where his individual actions within the ship formed part of a well-orchestrated fighting unit. As with most aspects of the Georgian navy, this was achieved through good organization. In addition to the Watch and Station Bill there was also a Quarter Bill, which listed where each man within the ship would work, or "close-up", when the ship went into action. The bill covered all men stationed at the guns, boarding parties, men working in the magazines, the teams passing powder and shot, those tending the wounded, manning pumps or fighting fires – the organization worked like a well-oiled machine.

Commencing with the guns, most seamen and marines were allocated to form individual gun crews. The crew of a gun were responsible for two guns, one on the larboard side of the ship and its opposite number on the starboard. The number of men allocated to a gun was determined by its weight and carriage; each man was expected to pull 500 pounds. For example, a 24-pounder gun weighing about 3 tons, had a gun crew of 12 men. However, if it was necessary to fire the guns on both sides of the ship simultaneously, then the gun's crew was split, with six men attending each gun. The limits on manpower were a matter of logistics: if the ship carried a full crew for every gun then the ship's complement would be doubled. This would create problems with accommodation on already cramped ships, and in provisioning. In a first-rate ship, such as the *Victory*, it would have meant carrying 44 per cent extra crew.

The standard gun's crew and duties for a 24-pounder gun are shown below. In addition to their

Gun's Crew for a 24-Pounder Gun

No.	Title	Task
1	Gun captain	Overall charge of the gun's crew and responsible for the safe loading, priming, firing and aiming of the gun.
1	Second gun captain	Pricked the cartridge and primed the gun. Took charge of the second gun on the opposite side of the ship. Manned the train tackle to haul gun back after firing.
1	Loader	Loaded cartridge, shot and wads. Manned the gun's side tackle to haul gun out into firing position.
1	Rammer	Rammed home cartridge, shot and wads. Manned the gun's side tackle to haul gun out into firing position.
1	Assistant rammer	Assisted ramming home cartridge, shot and wads. Manned the gun's side tackle to haul gun out into firing position.
1	Sponger	Swabbed gun with sponge after firing. Cleared gun with wadhook after every fourth firing. Manned the gun's side tackle to haul gun out into firing position.
1	Assistant sponger	Assisted swabbing gun with sponge after firing. Manned the gun's side tackle to haul gun out into firing position.
1	Powderman	Took charge of the salt box containing ready-use gunpowder cartridges and kept the box well clear behind the of the gun. Passed cartridges from salt box to the loader. If ship firing on both sides, the powderman became dedicated to both guns. This task was generally given to a marine. The powderman is not to be confused with "powder monkeys" (page 87).
4	Gun's crew	Manned the gun's side tackle to haul gun out into firing position. Manned the train tackle to haul gun back after firing.

Additional Duties For a 32-Pounder Gun's Crew

Letter	Task	No.
B	Boarders – to go on deck and repel or attack the enemy as required. These men would take up weapons, cutlasses, pikes, hatchets etc. from arms chest set out ready nearby. One of these men would be the marine allocated to the gun.	2
S	Sail trimmers – skilled seamen called upon to handle sails or brace the yards when manoeuvring.	2
P	Pumps – to man the pumps to discharge water flooding the hold through shot holes below the waterline.	2
F	Fire – to form part of a fire party operating the fire engine and its hoses or using buckets to douse fires within the ship.	1
L	Lanthorn – to hold the black lanthorn to provide safe light when fighting a night action.	1
	Total number removed in a worse case scenario	**8**
	Total remaining to operate the gun in a worse-case scenario	**6**

tasks at the gun, certain members of each gun's crew listed on the Quarter Bill were annotated by a letter, signifying other duties to meet particular circumstances in battle. A 32-pounder gun's crew of 14 men, for example, would be allocated duties as shown in the table above.

Depending on the rate of ship, each gun deck was controlled by one or two lieutenants, two midshipmen and a quarter gunner allocated to every four guns (eight guns if firing from both sides). Below in the main magazine would be the gunner or his assistant, the yeoman of the powder room and enough hands to fill "cases of wood" – the cylindrical cartridge boxes used to pass powder to the guns – and the ship's cooper, who broached the powder casks. The light-room, which illuminated the main magazine, was usually manned by the master-at-arms and the ship's cook. Other magazines were manned by the yeoman of the powder room who was assisted by a "non-combatant" such as a clerk or storeman. The carpenter and his crew would be below the waterline, armed with conical wooden plugs, sheets of lead, balls of oakum and nails, ready to stop up shot holes that penetrated the hull; their tasks were no different from the damage-control parties employed in modern warships.

The ship's captain, his first lieutenant, the master and the captain's clerk would be on the quarter deck recording events and signals. Not only was the quarter deck the place where the ship was steered, it was, in effect, the nerve centre from where the ship was directed in battle. The quarter deck would also contain a number of midshipmen who acted as communication officers to each respective deck. Because the quarter deck functioned as the command centre of the ship, it generally took the onslaught of the enemy fire during battle, the intention being to break down the chain of command within the ship and subsequently morale. This would explain why Nelson received his fatal wound at Trafalgar. It was not because he was visible by the decorations on his uniform, which being stitched to coat could not be removed anyway, it was simply as a result of him being there, and by the time he was shot, many others upon the quarter deck had either already been killed or sent below wounded. The smoke of battle would have masked the deck to some degree, therefore the French marksmen would simply target the area with blanket fire to cover all eventualities, and, statistically, it was extremely likely that Nelson would be hit.

The poop deck was manned by the signals officer, a midshipman and seamen ready to send or read signals from the rest of the fleet. Signal flags were held in special lockers at the after end of this deck. In ships without a poop, i.e. the frigate classes, the signal officer would be stationed on the quarter deck. Farther forward on the forecastle there would have been a midshipman and the boatswain with his crew, manning the guns and constantly ready with the anchors and their gear. Here the boatswain would have been ready to send men aloft to splice and knot rigging during the action to maintain the operation and safety of the rigging.

It has long been believed that cartridges were brought to the guns by the young boys universally referred to as "powder monkeys". While there is no argument about boys being involved in the transfer of powder, the practicalities of employing such a disorganized system has

"The Fall of Nelson" by Denis Dighton. While Nelson falls mortally wounded, midshipman Collingwood trains his musket to fire at where the fatal shot came from. To his left, a seaman carries a case of wood containing a cartridge.

to be questioned. Boys spending their entire time running to and from the magazines deep below in the ship would have been time consuming, open to failure by battle losses, and would have caused unnecessary congestion at magazine entrances when collecting the charges, especially when firing timed broadsides. The popular consensus that one boy was allocated to each gun is also false for crew lists show that the number of boys in any one ship did not meet even half the number of guns. The *Victory*, for example, had 100 guns but only 31 boys, and the 74-gun ships *Vanguard* and *Elephant* had 24 and 28 boys respectively. What is more, ship's standing orders, written by commanding officers at the time, clearly state that no boys were to be in, or near, the magazines; their main role is described as having to douse down loose powder around the guns. With their faces blackened with smoke and powder doing this task, it is easy to understand that the term "powder monkey" almost certainly originated from them being described as "black as monkeys".

Given that it is very unlikely that the well-administered Georgian navy would concede to using such an unmanageable system as described earlier, how were the powder charges really conveyed? Existing notebooks show that powder was passed via a chain of people stationed along the decks and passageways and at specific ladders and hatchways, and organized with specific routes to ensure that the right-sized charges reached the guns they were intended for; the results of inadvertently placing a charge for a 32-pounder gun in a 12-pounder gun are unimaginable. To accomplish powder transfer efficiently, some nine per cent of the crew would form the required lines passing the "cases of wood" containing the cartridges. In the first-rate ship *Victory*, this involved between 80 and 90 people. As for the boys, if they were employed during this process, they would have remained stationed on the gun decks, only taking the boxes from where they were passed up through the hatchways and using their natural agility to dodge through the gun's crews to supply the powdermen at each gun. Empty "cases of wood" were returned to the magazines for refilling via the same supply chain.

Preparing for Battle

During the French Revolutionary and Napoleonic Wars, preparing the ship for battle was practised frequently in English ships of war. Constantly exercising the ship's company did provide the English with an advantage over their adversaries. There is a distinct difference between the orders "clear ship for action" and "beat to quarters": the first relates to the ship and its equipment, the second is associated with the men. Unless the ship was a frigate, which by virtue of its layout could be quickly brought into action, preparation for battle within the larger ships was a little more involved than in smaller vessels. In 1797, the signal given for the fleet to clear for action was Number 53: "To Prepare for Battle." was given around 8am. On receiving this order, all the ships made their appropriate preparations, transforming the ships into a high state of battle readiness. Boatswains, with their shrill whistles, called all hands from below. Each man went to his station as directed by the Quarter Bill and, collectively, the entire ship was transformed into a formidable fortified battery. Ideally, a ship could be cleared for action within ten minutes, but because the time between sighting an enemy and actually closing with them was governed by wind conditions, the delay usually permitted the men to be stood down and await the next orders, which might be three hours later. At the appropriate moment the ship would "beat to quarters":

Nelson explains his intended battle tatics – termed the "Nelson Touch" – to his officers, before the battle of Trafalgar.

men stood to their guns and made final preparations. Clearing the ship for battle was centred around five main duties: clearing the decks; opening and preparing the magazines, powder and shot; unleashing the guns; adding safety rigging; and setting up an emergency operating theatre.

When clearing the decks, the first task was to extinguish the galley fire as a precautionary measure against fire and potential explosion from gunpowder. Livestock was either slaughtered or heaved overboard. All bulkheads and partitions forming cabins and compartments throughout the gun decks and under the poop were unshipped and taken below into the hold, hinged up and secured to the overhead beams out of the way, or, if time was at a premium, simply jettisoned overboard. Under the forecastle, the sick berth was also dismantled and those too incapacitated to provide any assistance were taken down to the orlop. Bulkheads were removed to provide more space for operating the guns, give better supervision of the gunnery, reduce risk of splinter damage to personnel, allow better ventilation, remove pockets of gunfire smoke and facilitate the free conveyance of both shot and powder. All bulkheads throughout the ship were either wooden panelled partitions; lightweight panels of canvas stretched over a slit-deal frame, which being cheap to make were considered expendable; or plain canvas screens made from old sailcloth nailed to the beams, which were either rolled up and tied secure or ripped down and discarded.

For similar reasons most of the pillars fitted between decks, which were not permanent fixtures, were knocked out with heavy mallets. Special beam jacks were sometimes used to assist their removal. All ladders considered unnecessary were unshipped and stowed below and rope scrambling nets were fitted in their place. Once all cabins, the gunroom, the galley pantry and sick berth were stripped out, all gun decks were left clear of most obstructions from stem to stern.

At the same time that bulkheads were being taken down, cabin furniture was also removed. By this period, most furniture carried on ships was of the "campaign" type, designed to break down into several portable sections or fold up for easy removal. It was then stowed within the hold below. Although it is popularly believed that furniture was placed into boats and towed astern, there is no evidence to suggest this. The captain commanding the 74-gun ship *Tonnant* at the battle of Trafalgar did use a wild plan as his ship sailed towards the enemy: he strung up Windsor chairs from the wardroom on a line rigged between her main and mizzen masts; her appearance must have raised a few French eyebrows as she bore down on them. All other manner of loose and unwarranted gear – chicken coops, etc. – was hurled overboard. The entry in the ship's log of the 74-gun *Orion* at the battle of Cape St. Vincent on 14 February 1797 states: "Clearing for action, lost overboard small tables 6. Canvas berths 4 thrown overboard. Butt staves, 750: Puncheon,

Plan showing Nelson's attack on the French fleet at the Battle of the Nile, 1 August, 1798.

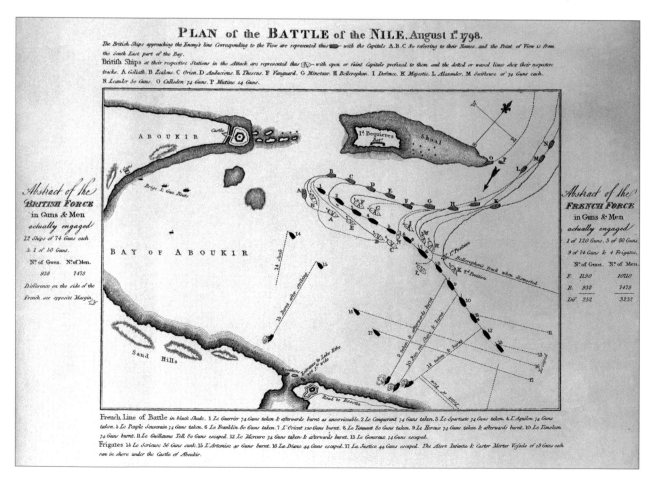

"Nelson's Inshore Blockading Squadron at Cadiz, July 1797" by Thomas Buttersworth.

ditto, 250: Hogsheads ditto, 180: Barrels 100: Iron hoops, 580 …" The *Orion*'s log also records that a steep tub containing 250 pieces of pork for the ship's company's dinner was later "shot to pieces". The item was either overlooked or left in anticipation of the battle's outcome.

All the seamen's hammocks were rolled up, brought on deck and stowed within the splinter (or hammock) nettings that surrounded the ship, where they formed a reasonable protective barricade for personnel against small arms fire and splinters. Once stowed, they were covered with canvas cloths, which, being a potential fire hazard, were wetted down prior to actual engagement. It was also common practice to lash some of the hammocks in the chains and the tops to protect the deadeyes and lanyards of the shrouds from enemy shot. Officer's cots were sent down into the hold along with the other furniture.

If the ship carried a fire engine, this was set up on deck with its hoses and nozzles. Pumps were manned to sluice the decks with water, after which they were sprinkled with sand. The decks were wetted to prevent potential fire or explosion from loose gunpowder and the sand provided better grip for the barefooted men when hauling on gun tackles. Leather fire buckets and wooden scuttles containing sand, and water buckets for swabs and for men to slake their thirst were placed behind each gun. To prevent flashback from explosions passing between decks, wetted canvas screens were rigged around hatchways. Emergency steering arrangements also had to be considered. Therefore extra tackle was rove to the tiller down in the gun room and a spare tiller was fitted into the rudder head at the level of the wardroom, complete with ropes and tackle.

The gunner and his mates (responsible for the magazines, powder and shot) would have unlocked the grand magazine and powder rooms, each of which were illuminated with special lanterns placed within their adjacent lightrooms for safety. In the grand magazine, hinged screens were swung up to let in light from the lightroom windows, which was covered by a copper grill. Before entering the magazines, certain precautionary measures were taken. Any clothing, belts, buckles or equipment containing steel were removed and footwear was replaced with felt slippers. Thick rough woollen "fearnought" or "dreadnought" screens furnished with a flap were nailed over the entry doors of all magazines and dampened down with water. By this period the passages leading to the grand magazine had lead-lined decks and the bulkheads forming these passages were laid up with lath and plaster work, the plaster acting as an anti-flash surface. The lead lining on the decks permitted the passage to be filled with an inch or so of water to deactivate loose gunpowder. Although there were many ready-use cartridges available, the gunner's assistants immediately started to make up more charges, measuring out the powder with copper scoops.

In the meantime, each gun captain went to the gunner's storeroom, where he was issued with a powder horn, spare gunlock flints, a length of slow match and linstock, cartridge prickers and vent reamers, a pouch containing quill firing tubes and spanners for adjusting the gunlocks. In some ships, gunlocks and their securing bolts were also issued if they were not already fitted to the gun. Other crew members collected arms chests containing muskets, pistols and cutlasses from the gun room and distributed their contents to each gunner. Each gun was issued with a salt box; these could contain two ready-use cartridges. Ready-use junk rope wads for the guns were either placed in nets strung from the beams along the centreline or sent up with the cartridges

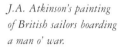

J.A. Atkinson's painting of British sailors boarding a man o' war.

inside the "cases of wood".

Up on deck, the boatswain and his mates busied themselves by carrying out measures that would prevent against damage to the ship's rigging and ensure that the ship's sailing capability was maintained. Such prerequisites were defined in Article VIII, Chapter III of the Regulations and Instructions, which outlined the boatswain's duties: "When the ship is preparing for battle, he is to be very particular in seeing that every thing necessary for repairing the rigging is in its proper place, that the men stationed to that service may know where to find immediately whatever may be wanted."

The brevity of this statement hides the reality of the work undertaken, for it involved rigging additional pendants and braces, called preventer braces, to the yards. In the case of the lower yards, the yard arm tackle, generally used for hoisting the ship's boats or stores, was adapted. The upper yards had extra pendants and braces rigged in readiness. They also rigged chain slings to support the lower yards in the event of the standard rope slings being shot through. To protect men from falling rigging and blocks, horizontal nets were rigged between the masts about 12 feet above deck level. Grappling hooks were suspended from the ends of the lower yards to lock into enemy rigging, while other grapnel irons with rope were laid around the upper decks ready for use in the event of boarding. As previously mentioned, hammocks were rigged to cover the deadeyes in the chains and tops. The boatswain also prepared spare cordage, tackle and tools for splicing severed ropes. He also took responsibility to ensure that cables and hawsers were prepared to cover any arising situation: to anchor the ship, to set up springs to veer the ship if anchored, or to take a ship in tow. Canvas and twine were also arranged for patching sails.

The carpenter and his mates would also have been on this deck making provision for stopping up shot holes between "wind and water". Their equipment comprised wooden plugs, sheets of lead, nails, tarred canvas and tallow, along with suitable tools. This practice had been in force since the time of Queen Elizabeth I.

As busy as everyone was, preparation throughout the ship was done in complete silence – a fact that was later remarked upon by Napoleon as he was being transported aboard the *Bellerophon* to exile. Once all the preparations were complete and the first lieutenant was satisfied, and provided that the enemy was still distant, the men were stood down, given their spirits and fed, usually while still at their guns. As soon as battle became imminent, the crew were sent to "quarters". According to the logbook of the *Colossus* at the battle of Cape St. Vincent: "At 11 the Admiral made the signal to form the line ahead and astern as convenient. Piped to Dinner. Served part of the ship's company … At half past 11 the Orion began. Beat to Quarters. Had no time to strike the wine down, therefore hove the cask overboard with 58 gallons of wine…"

When ordered to "quarters", the ship's drummer would beat out a rapid staccato, probably "Heart of Oak". Everything was dropped as the men raced to their stations. Those not operating guns formed the chain leading from the magazines to the decks to pass the powder charges, others went to the hold to start passing shot up from their lockers. If it had not already been done when clearing for action, the order "cast loose your guns" was given and each gun crew unleashed their guns from the stowed position. Tompions, the wooden plugs fitted into the gun muzzles, and aprons were removed, the latter exposing the gunlocks. Gun port lids were opened by the order "level your guns", after which quoins and beds were inserted under the breech of each of the guns and were adjusted to range the guns point blank. On receipt of the order "run out your guns", crews manning the side tackles hauled their guns into the firing position. No loading was required as all guns were already loaded in a constant state of readiness. The cartridge within the gun was pricked and quill firing tubes were inserted into the vent leaving the gun ready for final priming. The gun's side arms, comprising rammers, sponges and wadhhooks, were taken down from their overhead racks.

Firing and Reloading the Guns

Each gun captain, fussing like a mother over her child, made his final adjustments to the gun. After setting the gunlock to its half-cocked (safe) position, he filled the pan of the gunlock with powder from his powder horn and, after leaving more powder on the vent pan for good measure, removed the tallow cap from the firing tube. Awaiting the final order to fire, he fully cocked the gunlock and called to his gun's crew to "make ready", which signalled to his gun's crew to position themselves clear of the gun carriage and its trucks to avoid be struck by the gun as it recoiled when fired. By this point, the gun captain was standing well behind his gun with the trigger lanyard for the gunlock ready in hand. On the order to fire, he tugged that trigger line and the gun belched its missile towards the enemy. Reacting to its discharge, the gun recoiled into the ship, coming to a violent stop as it reached the full extent of the breeching rope that was securing it to the ship's side.

The gun captain then gave the order to "sponge out": the sponger and his assistant inserted the dampened sheep-wool sponge into the gun's muzzle and forced it down the bore to douse any remaining embers left from the charge, whilst the second gun captain was "stopping" the vent all the while with his thumb to prevent hazardous burning embers from escaping. After scouring the gun the spongers then withdrew the sponge – the vacuum created by virtue of the vent being "thumbed" ensured that any remaining burning debris was extinguished.

On the gun captain's order "load with cartridge", the powderman passed the cartridge to the loader, who then inserted it into the muzzle of the gun. Aided by his assistant, he rammed the charge home. The gun captain then checked it by inserting his cartridge pricker down the vent. His next order, "load with shot", was given and the loader inserted the round shot, which was rammed home as before. "Wad the gun", was ordered and the same loading sequence followed.

With the gun loaded, the gun captain then shouted, "run out the gun", and, as before, the gun's crew hauled the guns into the firing position. Pushing the cartridge pricker down the vent, the second gun captain spiked the cartridge, exposing the gunpowder, after which he inserted a new quill firing tube into the vent and removed its tallow cap. The gun captain half cocked the gunlock, checked the striking edge of the flint, filled the gunlock pan with powder and added a small train of powder on the vent. He fully cocked the gunlock and called his gun's crew to "make ready". The breeching rope and side tackle ropes were cleared away from the carriage and its trucks and the crew stood back. When ordered to do so, the gun captain fired the gun.

Although the gun drill proved highly efficient under normal sea conditions, the gun's crew had to adjust their routine if the ship was rolling heavily. If the gun was fired on a downward roll, the recoil motion would be reduced as the gun forced its way back up the deck. In these circumstances, it may have been necessary to haul the gun back to its reload position using the train tackle fitted at the rear of the carriage. Under the same conditions, the seamen would use the train tackle to prevent the gun from rolling forward when it was being reloaded.

Discipline and Punishment

Recent research and analysis has shown that many of the preconceived ideas about discipline and punishment within the Georgian navy need to be put into the context of the period concerned. Discipline – the practice applied to attain good authoritative organization – should not be confused with its counterpart, punishment. Admiral Collingwood's statement, "Nothing is achieved without order or discipline", encapsulates the essential requirements of ship management. Any breakdown of order or discipline could result in the total loss of the ship, damage or loss of equipment, unnecessary injury or death, or the failure to engage an enemy. Punishment – the means to maintain that order and discipline – was readily accepted by both officers and seamen alike.

Punishment was harsh, but no more so than was expected on land during the Georgian period. If punishment was so awful then why, during the Great Mutiny of 1797, did the seamen not raise this aspect as a major point of grievance when petitioning the Admiralty with more pressing demands? Furthermore, while the ships were under the control of the seamen during the mutiny, discipline was fully maintained under the boatswains and other petty officers, and harsh punishment continued to be handed out when necessary. Unfortunately, many of the myths surrounding punishment derive from the works of the naval reformers of the 1830s, who embellished tales of the actions of the previous regime in order to justify their own idealized cause. Historical records show that as the war with France became more prolonged the Admiralty and its officers were increasingly faced with crews made up of conscripts and other non-professional seaman. The result was that punishment had to be administered more frequently in order to maintain authority when discipline deteriorated. This does not mean that punishment became unjust, merely that tolerance had lessened.

All persons serving in the navy were subject to two statute sets of Admiralty rules: the Articles of War and the Regulations and Instructions Relating to His Majesty's Service at Sea. The Articles of War, which originated in the 1650s, were revised during the reign of Charles II and further amended in 1749 and 1757 by the parliament of George II, covered 36 separate laws together with their corresponding penalties. The foremost article formalized that all commanding officers were to uphold the Christian religion and conduct divine service on Sunday. The remainder covered all points concerning failure of duty, espionage, cowardice and conduct appertaining to the service and moral issues – most of these articles carried the death penalty. In all, the Articles of War provided the means by which the captain of any ship held supreme power over his crew. It was common practice for the captain to read out the Articles of War to the entire ship's company when taking commission of a ship. When Captain Richard Peacock took command of the 80-gun *Foudroyant* on Monday 24 November 1806 he "Joined the Ship and read his Commission and the Articles of War." After this the Articles were read to a ship's company at least twice a month after

Midshipman seized up the shrouds as a punishment. Why an animal is shown in the right hand gun port is a mystery.

divine service had been held, the objective being to remind all concerned of their position. When punishment was given, the section of the Articles that related to the crime would also be read to the ship's crew, again as a warning. Revised many times to comply with social changes, the Articles of War still hold authority within the navy today.

First introduced in 1731 and revised in 1787, the Admiralty Regulations and Instructions Relating to His Majesty's Service at Sea were contained in a volume comprising 440 pages. These instructions covered the more general day-to-day issues of management and duties of personnel, such as routine, storekeeping and related accounts, including those of the purser, boatswain, gunner and carpenter. Supporting these guidelines were Captain's Orders, which spelled out definite regulations, duties and routines that related directly to the ship on which he had command. By 1807, such orders became standardized throughout the fleet, yet each still carried specific additions instigated at the discretion of the commanding officers. These orders are called Ship's Standing Orders today.

Serious offences, which carried a penalty of either death, imprisonment, dismissal from the service or floggings of more than two dozen lashes, were dealt with by a court martial. For this the captain of the ship had to make a request to his commander-in-chief to convene a court comprising a minimum of five senior officers and admirals to try the defendant who, under such circumstances, was allowed a counsel. Although logbooks show that court martials were held quite regularly, this did not mean that men were invariably found guilty: quite the contrary, most were acquitted because of mitigating circumstances. If a ship was lost, holding a court martial against the entire crew was automatic. Indeed, even admirals were not exempt from such trials.

The death penalty for petty officers, seamen and marines meant hanging. This was always carried out on the ships to which they belonged, with the execution being carried out by their fellow men. Prior to the execution, a gun was fired calling for an officer from each ship to witness the event, the officer concerned embarked in a boat "manned and armed". The company of each ship of the fleet was also called to their decks to witness the affair. With his head covered with a hood, the victim stood on the larboard side with the noose ready around his neck. Signalled by a second gun, some 20 seamen ran aft with the rope and "hoisted the man into eternity" from the block hanging at the larboard yard-arm of the fore lower yard where it remained for an hour before being lowered. Officers were executed by a firing squad.

The punishment beneath that of a death sentence was flogging around the fleet, where a man could be given between 100 and 1,000 lashes. Tied to two capstan bars erected in a boat, the unfortunate victim was rowed from ship to ship where he received a number of lashes, the quantity varying according to the number of ships in the squadron. The boat contained a drummer, who played a rogue's march, plus officers and armed marines from the offender's ship. A surgeon was also present and he would stop the punishment if the victim's life seemed threatened. Under such circumstances, the remainder of the punishment would be deferred until the man was medically fit enough to receive the outstanding number of lashes. It was not uncommon for some men to die from this punishment, hence such a sentence was generally reserved for deserters who did not have mitigating circumstances. On one occasion in 1798 when two seamen were being flogged, 200 of the crew watching the event on the 74-gun ship *Mars* fell over the ship's side when the rail gave way. Many were injured.

Most punishments were confined to flogging within the ship; the punishment authorized by the commanding officer. Officially no captain could award more than one dozen lashes without seeking higher authority, which invariably required a court martial, and while this may have applied in the earlier parts of the war, sentences actually increased after 1800. Floggings, using a cat-o'-nine-tails, were always witnessed by the entire ship's company, the offender being tied to an upturned grating at the fore end of the quarter deck. All marines, armed with loaded muskets and fixed bayonets, would be lined up as a precautionary measure against possible insurrection. However, as flogging was a common

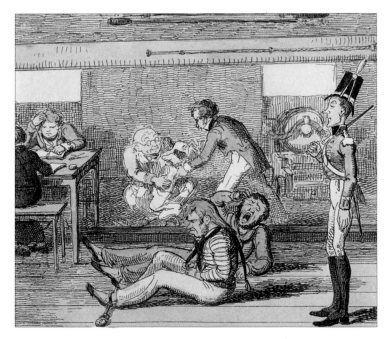

"In Irons for getting Drunk" by George Cruickshank. If agressive, seamen were constrained in the bilboes while awaiting a flogging.

occurrence of the time, this was quite unlikely. Before punishment commenced, the captain would read out the name of the offender, his charge and sentence and the relevant part of the Articles of War appertaining to the crime.

Although punishment was swift, decisive and, in most cases, quite just, it did not occur every day, as we are often led to believe. By 1800 it was becoming quite common for captains to carry out punishment weekly, utilizing the event to have a number of men flogged rather than one or two, to make a statement. This is clearly shown in the logbooks of the frigate *La Minerve*, the 80-gun *Foudroyant* and the 100-gun *Victory*.

Close examination of original records shows traits in breach of discipline that generally correspond to altering situations. The most common was that boredom of blockade duty often destroyed morale and affected discipline, likewise disciplinary problems arose within the ships in the aftermath of the battle. After the Battle of Copenhagen on 1 April 1801, three marines serving on the *Raisonnable* were each flogged with 24 lashes for "mutinous behaviour", while on the

Punishment given by Captain George Cockburn on *La Minerve* – 19 March 1799

Name	Rank	Offence	No. of Lashes
William Tupper	Marine	Fighting	12
James Hanrahan	Marine	Fighting	12
John Thomas	Seaman	Fighting	36
George Smith	Seaman	Fighting	36
Thomas Isaac	Seaman	Insolence	12
Redman Welch	Seaman	Theft	96
John Harrison	Seaman	Sleeping on his post	24
John Welstead	Seaman	Drunkenness	12

Note: Research shows that Redman Welch was a habitual thief who, irrespective of previous severe punishment, did not appear to have learned to stop thieving, hence the high number of lashes. John Thomas and John Welstead were also repeated offenders.

Punishment given by Captain Edward Berry on the *Foudroyant* – 22 March 1800

Name	Rate	Offence committed	No. of lashes
John Credit	Seaman	Insolence and drunkenness	36
Thomas Barnwell	Seaman	Drunkenness	36
George James	Seaman	Drunk on duty and stealing the ship's wine	36
James Parnell	Seaman	Leaving the boat on duty	36
William Meacham	Marine	Drunkenness and sleeping on his post	36
Paul McDonald	Seaman	Fighting	24
James Sangster	Seaman	Leaving the boat on duty	24
John Mongell	Seaman	Insolence	24
Total Lashes Given			**252**

Punishment given by Captain Thomas Masterman Hardy on the *Victory* – July 1804

Date	Name	Rate	Offence	No. of lashes
Tues. 3 July	William Inwood	Boatswain's Mate	Theft	48
Tues. 3 July	Anthony Antonio	Cook's Mate	Disobedience of orders	36
Tues. 3 July	Thomas Palmer	Seaman	Drunkenness	36
Tues. 3 July	Daniel Sweeny	Marine	Contempt and drunkenness	36
Tues. 3 July	John Brice	Marine	Neglect of duty	12
Tues. 10 July	Patrick Merryan	Seaman	Drunkenness	36
Tues. 10 July	Peter Mcgee	Seaman	Drunkenness and fighting	48
Tues. 10 July	Thomas Maloney	Seaman	Drunkenness and fighting	48
Tues. 10 July	Samuel Baker	Marine	Sleeping at his post	24
Tues. 24 July	Henry Butcher	Seaman	Theft	48
Tues. 24 July	Joseph Brown	Seaman	Insolence	24
Tues. 24 July	John Jacobs	Seaman	Fighting	24
Tues. 24 July	John Brown	Seaman	Drunkenness	24
Tues. 24 July	Thomas Thomas	Seaman	Fighting	12
Tues. 24 July	Henry Thompson	Seaman	Fighting	24
Tues. 24 July	John Thomas	Seaman	Insolence and disobedience of orders	24

Elephant, Captain Foley had similar problems. Between the 17 April and 18 May 1801 he punished nine seamen and five marines for drunkenness – the total lashes between them amounting to 252 – while another seaman received 12 lashes for disobedience and neglect, and a marine received 12 for neglect.

As in all groups in society, there was always a minority of people who consistently flouted the rules; regardless of how many times they were punished, they continuously disobeyed. One crime that was not tolerated was theft, which usually warranted greater punishment on account of the fact that it was a crime that affected morale and trust among the crew. Also not tolerated was physical violation or injury towards other men. For example, one man on the *Victory* received: "Eighteen lashes for drunkenness, cutting down a man in his hammock and beating him"; another man, punished on the same day, only got 12 lashes for desertion.

The most common offence was drunkenness, or other crimes instigated by drink. For the seamen this was, in some respects, both unfortunate and unfair, especially when they were issued with more than adequate quantities of wine, beer and rum. Two sources, the logbooks of the *Foudroyant* and the *Victory*, provide sound evidence of this problem. More noteworthy is that ten men were flogged on the *Victory* just two days before the battle of Trafalgar.

Discipline commonly appears to have broken down when the ship was not at sea. This is primarily because the seamen were not in sea watches and were therefore less occupied. Marines, on the other hand, tended to be more of a problem at sea than when they were actively employed whilst the ship was in harbour. This situation began to improve as the 18th century drew to a close, however, as marines became recognized as a fighting unit rather than being seen as Regiments of Foot sent to sea. Geographical location, too, had its effect on discipline. Existing ship's logs show that the percentage of punishment administered for drunkenness, desertion or neglect while ships were stationed in the West Indies was always higher than elsewhere. Port Royal, with its exotic attractions, proved to be a greater temptation for the seamen as well as for the marines, who were generally more reliable.

Other punishments included "running the gauntlet", where the offender, usually caught for theft, had to pass around the deck through lines of the assembled crew who would each lash out at the man with a knotted rope end. Less tolerated by the seamen was the informal punishment indiscriminately handed out by officers, midshipmen and petty officers during the normal course of their duties. Colloquially termed as "starting", this usually took the form of being beaten around the head and shoulders with a specially prepared rope end or a rattan cane. Although formally abolished in 1809, this wretched practice did persist. Midshipmen were punished by caning, being tied up in the mizzen's shrouds for long periods, or they were mast-headed – sent aloft to the crosstrees at the head of the topmast where they had to remain in the wind and cold until finally called back on deck.

Music and Leisure

Music, it appears, was one of the few forms of relaxation in which the sailors took part – mainly, as Samuel Leech states in his memoirs, "to drive away dull care." The most common instruments – the fiddle, fife and flute – could each be safely stored within a crowded man o' war. Any seaman knowing a good repertoire of tunes and ballads was very much appreciated by the men, who would, it is reported, "sing in their hammocks of an evening". Although most songs were of a melancholic nature, the men also danced happily to the gay tunes played by a fiddler. Dancing was much encouraged by captains because it eased morale and gave the men some exercise.

Unfortunately very few tunes and songs of the period survive today. Contrary to popular belief, few of the sea-shanties that are well known today have any connection with the Nelsonian period; most actually derived from seamen serving in the merchant fleet of the mid 19th century and later. Most songs sung by the seamen were equally popular on land, the most well known being "Drops of Brandy", which originated from an old country-dance tune. The words that accompanied this tune were as follows:

"Third Officer's Mess Room" by Charles Copland. Note the gun lashed for sea, portable canvas and deal bulkhead screens, a Pembroke table, and folding canvas stools.

And Johnny shall have a new bonnet,
And Johnny shall go to the fair,
And Johnny shall have a blue ribbon
To tie up his bonny brown hair.
And why should I not love Johnny?
And why should not Johnny love me?
And why should I not love Johnny
As well as another body?

Other popular songs included "Nancy Dawson" and "Spanish Ladies" – the latter

was already quite an old song, even in Nelson's day. "Spanish Ladies" epitomizes the nostalgic feeling of men returning from fighting with large Spanish ships (the "Spanish Ladies" of the song's title) or from blockade duty off Spain as they pass the familiar headlands and landmarks along the English Channel before arriving in the Downs – the safe anchorage between Deal and the Goodwin Sands. Having arrived and anchored, the men relaxed by drinking great bumpers of beer and spirits. The modern equivalent, made popular by the folk group The Spinners in the 1970s would be "Whip Jamboree", which also lists known headlands. Another song of Irish origin, "Fine Girl You Are", was frequently sung by the British sailors that manned the frigates that formed the fishery protection squadron operating out of Londonderry in the early 1960s.

It is often thought that a fiddler would have been employed to play a jaunty tune while men were manning the capstan. Unfortunately this may not have been the case because most work was done in absolute silence , while most capstan orders – i.e. haul, veer and pause – were given by distinguishable "calls" that were made by the boatswain's mates on their pipes. If a fiddle was being played, their whistles would not have been clearly heard. Some captains did encourage men to form a ship's band, mainly to entertain the officers, and it was not uncommon to hear the tones of "The Roast Beef of Old England" being played when the officers went to dinner. Bands were also used to relieve the men's nerves as they went into battle. At Trafalgar, the British ships sailed towards the enemy with bands playing "Rule Britannia", "Heart of Oak", "Britons Strike Home" and other jingoistic airs.

Besides reading – and few men other than the officers had the opportunity to read, not so much through lack of literacy as because of a lack of books – there was little other recreation for

"Sailors Carousing" by George Cruickshank. This scene encapsulates the boisterous secenes of depravity found in a shore-side alehouse – a much-favoured haunt of seamen.

the seamen to relieve their boredom. Some of them would take up some form of handicraft, while the more literate kept journals. The journals that have survived provide a fascinating insight into the daily activities aboard a ship of war. Most simply sat around in groups, repairing their clothing while talking about their past ships or other incidents; most of these stories would have been embellished to excite the listeners. Seamen pressed into service from one trade or other would often exploit their skills to supplement their pay. A cobbler, for example, would make or repair shoes for the crew, while a tailor would produce jackets, trousers, etc. Although discouraged, gambling, using playing cards or dice, would also exist.

Plays of various sorts were occasionally staged, complete with costumes acquired by different means. One Trafalgar ship actually kept a wardrobe of dresses and other female attire for just such occasions. After the battle, the "stage" clothing was used to re-cloth Jeanette, a French woman who had lost all of her clothes when escaping from the burning ship *Achille*.

It appears that the men that manned the Georgian ships were not adverse to carrying out various pranks to alleviate the monotonous routine and confined existence. Moreover, these pranks were not, as Commander James Gardner recalls in his memoirs, just confined to the boisterous midshipmen. Drinking, it appears, was an all-too-common means of relaxation for both officers and seamen alike. For the seamen this is reflected in the logbooks and punishment returns of the period, as most "crimes" were drink related. Alternatively, men used tobacco, which after 1798 was issued free at two pounds per month. While most men would chew their tobacco, those that did smoke used small clay pipes. Because of fire risk below decks, and the fact that guns were always loaded, smoking was confined to the forecastle or next to the galley, where the deck was lined with brick. Contemporary illustrations also show that seamen and marines fished using a rod and line; one logbook actually states that rods, lines and hooks were issued to the men to encourage this sport, the catch obviously used to supplement their diet.

Shore leave was often only granted to the most trusty seamen and men of higher ranks: most of the crew were confined to the ship in harbour through fear that they might desert. To satisfy natural desires, women were allowed onto the ships and lived on the crowded decks with the men. Officially, at least, this was restricted to the "wives of the men they come to; and the ship be not too much pestered even with them". In reality, however, the rules were ignored and all manner of women indulged with the men. On the 74-gun

Seamen carousing with women on board ship while in harbour.

ship *Revenge*, which had a crew of 600, Jack Nastyface reports that 450 women went on board, most of whom were in all likelihood prostitutes. Nastyface adds that: "On arrival of a man-of-war in port, these girls flock down to the shore, where boats are always ready; and here may be witnessed a scene somewhat similar to the trafficking in slaves in the West Indies." One officer, remarking on the lack of privacy below decks, stated: "The whole of the shocking, disgraceful transactions of the lower deck it is impossible to describe, the dirt, filth, and stench; the disgusting conversation; the indecent, beastly conduct and horrible scenes; the blasphemy and swearing; the riots, quarrels and fighting … squeezed between the next hammocks and must be witness to each other's actions … giving way to every excess and debauchery that the grossest passions of human nature can lead to." While all might seem highly degrading, and open to criticism, the practice of having women on board was very much accepted. What is remarkable is that there is no reference in any of the official logbooks regarding the embarkation of women onto the ships while they were in harbour.

Women, many of whom were the wives of the warrant officers, did serve on ships. Besides those who cross-dressed to avoid detection – the marine Hannah Snell for example – others simply remained hidden. At the Battle of the Nile, a woman on board the *Tremendous* gave birth in the heat of battle, the boy being christened David Tremendous McKenzie, while at the Battle of Copenhagen there were 11 women serving on board the 74-gun ship *Bellona*. In most cases they helped passing powder or tending to the wounded. However, one woman, recorded in seaman John Pearce's journal, was actually serving as part of a gun's crew on board the *Prince George* at the Battle of Saintes in 1782, until "shot through her Arm some dangerously" by a musket ball.

VICTUALLING AND HEALTH AT SEA

Nobody can deny the fact that life at sea could never be as comfortable as that on land. This is as true today as it was around 1800. The sea is an untamed mass that can create a hostile environment, alienating man from his natural habitat. Aside from the state of the ships themselves, man's limited mastery over the sea is dependent on three basic requirements: seamanship, provisions and health. Elements of seamanship have been discussed elsewhere; the other two requirements, which are fully reliant on good organization, will be looked at here.

Provisions

From a 21st century perspective, it is often believed that living on a Georgian naval vessel was a terrible experience of hardship, made worse by an intolerable organization that carried out cruel retribution at every opportunity. Unfortunately we have all too regularly been presented with the picture that victualling and diet in the Georgian navy was lacking. This is a misconception, mainly due to over-exuberant embellishment from both fiction writers and sailors' yarns, complacent historians of the late 19th and early 20th centuries, and television and film directors seeking to sensationalize the facts. Contrary to popular belief, Georgian seamen generally fared far better than their civilian counterparts.

Standard Rations Per Man

Day	Bread lbs.	Beer pints	Beef lbs.	Pork lbs.	Pease pints	Oatmeal pints	Butter ounces	Cheese ounces
Sunday	I	8	—	I	—	—	—	—
Monday	I	8	—	—	—	I	2	4
Tuesday	I	8	2	—	—	—	—	—
Wednesday	I	8	—	—	—	I	2	4
Thursday	I	8	—	I	—	—	—	—
Friday	I	8	—	—	—	I	2	4
Saturday	I	8	2	—	—	—	—	—
Weekly Total	**7**	**56**	**4**	**2**	**2**	**3**	**6**	**12**
Weekly (metric)	3.2 kg	32 ltr	1.8 kg	0.9 kg	1.1 ltr	1.7 ltr	0.8 kg	0.34 kg

NOTE: The above are the basic rations only and could be supplemented with raisins and vegetables. An equivalent amount of flour could have been substituted for bread.

Operating a sailing man o' war with little or no mechanical aids was an extremely labour-intensive occupation, requiring a diet high enough in calories to fuel this degree of physical work. Consequentially, the daily food intake for each crew member needed to contain between 4,500 and 5,000 calories, an amount not dissimilar to that required by farm labourers, especially during the harvest season.

No commanding officer could possibly have expected his ship to run in an organized and efficient manner if his crew were undernourished. The fact that the Georgian navy was generously provisioned is well documented from the information shown in surviving ships' logbooks. Nobody disputes that the diet was extremely monotonous, but this was largely due to the fact that obviously only certain provisions could be carried for long periods. A typical storing list, such as that for the 74-gun ship *Theseus* between 15 March and 23 May 1810, would be as shown in the table opposite.

Dry Provisions

Item	Quantity
Bread (ship's biscuits)	78,450 lbs
Butter	939 lbs
Cabbage	394 lbs
Cheese	1,801 lbs
Flour	2,352 lbs
Fresh Beef	11,866 lbs
Greens	808 lbs
Leeks	417 lbs
Oatmeal	1,248 lbs
Potatoes	2,615 lbs
Suet	306 lbs
Sugar	840 lbs
Total weight	**101,991 lbs**
Total weight	**45.53 tons**

NOTE: This list omits salted pork and beef which would already have been stored.

Fluids

Item	Quantity
Beer	6,745 galls
Rum	4,897 galls
Vinegar	707 galls
Water	33,525 galls
Wine	2,801 galls
Total gallons	48,675 galls
Total weight	486,750 lbs
Total weight	**217.30 tons**
Total weight dry and fluid stores	**262.83 tons**

Meat which was preserved in salt and packed into casks, was stored in this way for use on land as well as at sea. Each cask of meat, whether beef or pork, generally contained about 56 pieces; each piece of beef weighed about eight pounds, while each piece of pork was four pounds in weight. These weights equated to standard Irish meat measures. A cask of salted meat, the equivalent to our tinned food today, was mainly used when alternative stocks either could not be acquired or when they had run out. The fact that fresh meat, either on the bone or in the form of livestock, was obtained at every opportunity to supplement the preserved meats, can be clearly ratified by many logbooks. On examination, the quantities of fresh meat provided while ships lay off harbour was quite high. The captured frigate *La Minerve*, for example, received a total of 2,652 pounds of fresh beef over a seven-day period in October 1798. Given that her ship's company only comprised 300 men, each person would have received a ration of nearly nine pounds during this period. Fresh meat "for the ship's company" received on board the *Foudroyant* between 18 and 25 May 1809 amounted to 1,380 pounds equating to two pounds per head. Four oxen, weighing 494, 384, 444 and 475 pounds each, were slaughtered for fresh meat on board the *Agamemnon* while she was operating off the Leeward Islands between 20 and 23 March 1806.

Popular opinion suggests that all livestock were kept within an area called the "manger", located at the fore end of the gun deck. Partitioned by manger boards, which formed a bulkhead across the deck about four feet high, its real purpose was to prevent sea water, which entered through the hawse holes when they were not plugged, from running the full length of the deck. While this may seem a suitable place to keep animals in most ships, it was totally impractical due to the difficulties of loading some six to ten head of cattle or sheep through two or three decks. In the interests of hygiene and crew health, it is also unlikely that surgeons would have encouraged such a practice. Today's misconception probably developed from literary sources where a writer familiarized himself with life at sea by sailing in a frigate-classes ship where the manger was located at the fore end of the single gun deck not far from the open waist. Loading livestock down through the waist and moving them to the manger was far easier on such ships. It must also be remembered that seamen in the frigate classes were not berthed on the gun deck, but further

This caricature shows chickens and carrots and other vegetables being prepared. As seen here, the crew members were multi racial.

below on a berthing deck and would, therefore, have been segregated from the animals. Also, due to crew size of frigates, fewer animals would have been contained. The term "manger" derives from the French verb *manger,* meaning to eat, hence the function of the manger was to contain fodder, not animals. This is supported by the account of the loss of the *Boyne*, which caught fire when the hay held within the manger spontaneously combusted. Livestock was generally penned within a temporary corral built by the ship's carpenter.

Bread – the term used for ship's biscuits – was either packed in sacks or casks. Another popular misconception is that this always contained weevils and maggots. Weevils can be found in flour even today, but being so minute they simply blend during the cooking process. Ship's biscuits were cooked twice during preparation to render them impervious for long-term storage; it was only when the "bread" became damp that it began to deteriorate and become infested. Logbooks suggest that bread was regularly inspected and discarded and was periodically "picked" by the crew to eliminate deteriorating supplies. The log of the *Seahorse* of March 1775, for example, states that "Master, Boatswain and Gunner of his Majesty's Ship Coventry came on board and Surveyed some damaged bread which they found as follows Viz. Bread Two Thousand five hundred and Sixty Pound, damp, full of Vermin and unfit for Men to eat, occasioned in their opinions by the bread being damp."

Dried fish, much used before the middle of the 18th century, had ceased to be carried because it went rotten quickly. All foodstuffs were inspected, weighed or counted by the purser, master and officer of the watch before daily issue, and any deficiency or actions regarding the disposal of unfit items resulting from this inspection were recorded within the ship's log. Comments such as "opened a cask of beef no. 266 from Plymouth containing 54 pieces found short seven pieces" and "found a cask of bread considered unfit for a man to eat and discharged it overboard by Order" are common. Such cases were recorded for two reasons: to set the purser's accounts straight so that he could claim back 50 per cent of the cost, and to highlight the discrepancies made by the appropriate Victualling Yard or supplier to the Navy Board. It was due to such deficiencies that pursers were often wrongly perceived as being fraudulent scoundrels, when in truth most procured provisions in good faith.

By the end of the 18th century, the problem of scurvy, a disease caused by a deficiency of vitamin C, which had plagued seamen for centuries, had almost been eliminated. This was conquered by introducing lemons, limes and onions into the diet, and by procuring fresh vegetables at every opportunity. This shows that progress was now being made in understanding the necessity of a good balance in diet, with the result that the seamen became far healthier. When the 74-gun ship *Vanguard* was preparing to leave Naples on 23 July 1799 she embarked: "10 Bulocks {sic}, 3,000 Onions, 510 Cabbages and 520 lbs of fresh Beef." A month later while at Port Mahon, the same ship took on board: "15 casks of pease, 15 casks of oatmeal, 2 casks of suet, 3 casks of raisins, 10 firkins of butter and 561 pound of fresh beef."

A 200-year old ship's biscuit. Baked twice for hardening, such biscuits could last indefinitely, provided they were kept dry.

Livestock was not, as is often believed, fresh meat for the sole use of the officers but, as most logbooks show, for the seamen. The log of the *Theseus*, for example, states that in January 1795 they "killed two bullocks and issued to the ships Co. 703 lbs Fresh Beef." The damp environment was not the only cause of food deterioration: *Vanguard*'s log of 31 August 1799 records that they "found a Cask of Pease No. 36 ... and a Cask of Rice Cts. [contents] 465 lbs totally destroyed by the rats". The same ship, this time anchored off Landserona in the Baltic in May 1808 received from transports "1,288 pounds fresh beef 350 lbs vegetables". *Vanguard* also received 505 gallons of rum, 588 pounds of sugar

and 417 pounds of cocoa from the 74-gun ship *Orion*.

These log entries, and many others like them, clearly indicate that the general diet in the Royal Navy had improved simply because of the fact that the proportion of meat to vegetables had at least reached a ratio of three to one, whereas the seamen's diet had contained virtually no vegetables at the beginning of the wars in 1793. As their dietary importance was realized, we see that the quantities of vegetables steadily increased after 1800; on arrival at Plymouth from South America on 6 November 1812, the 80-gun *Foudroyant* took on board 2,400 pounds of fresh beef and 1,600 pounds of vegetables – a ratio now of three to two.

Records also show that ships serving in the East Indies, based at Madras or Bombay, commonly embarked rice as an alternative to European cereals because of its abundant availability and cost. In all, standard provisions were highly substituted with suitable local produce. Warships regularly provisioned each other as is shown from the records of many ships. One such case involved the 39-gun frigate *L'Unité*, which when deployed in the West Indies in 1799, operating off the island of Nevis on 25 July, supplied the 16-gun sloop *Favorite* with the following: "Provisions. Viz Bread 986 lb Wine 86 gall, Rum 41 1/2 [gallons], Beef 528 lb, Pork 488 lb, Pease 80 [lb], Flour 515 lb, Sugar 41 lb." After getting into Fort Royal two days later, the *L'Unité* naturally had to re-provision again before sailing for Surinam three days later.

The wars with France meant that ships had to be deployed for longer periods at sea and storage capacity was therefore restricted. Besides embarking four to six months' worth of stores and provisions before sailing on deployment, naval ships during Nelson's period were also provisioned at sea. Since the Seven Years' War (1756–63), it had long been the practice to replenish ships at sea by maintaining a well-organized fleet of transport and victualling vessels that continuously sailed to and from the dockyards and victualling yards and various supply stations – Corsica, Gibraltar and Malta, for example.

The transport service operated in exactly the same way as the vessels that form the Royal Fleet Auxiliary Service do today, except that in Nelson's time the transports and victualling ships were hired in as required rather than being maintained as a permanent auxiliary service. Besides carrying new stores, all empty casks that had contained meat, peas, butter etc. were returned to the victualling yards via these transports. In most cases, the barrels prepared for return were "shaken down"; staves were bundled together, hoops were bundled separately, and then transferred – the quantities were all recorded. Not only did the transports carry standard solid provisions, they also served as water tenders. While in most cases provisions were transferred from ship to ship by launch, it is not unfeasible that some simple form of direct ship-to-ship transfer using ropes was used; considering the seamen's skills, the use of such a system seems quite probable.

During the transfer, the empty water casks were embarked onto the transport ships which then sailed for the nearest base to refill them.Besides foodstuffs, ships needed to restock with fresh supplies of water, rum, beer or wine. Captains of ships would replenish supplies of fresh water at every opportunity. As soon as the ship came to anchor, its boats were immediately lowered and sent on shore with empty casks for refilling. Water and other fluid requirements were also constantly supplied from transport ships, especially frigates rejoining the fleet.

The *Victory*'s records show that in the first two weeks of August 1803, while blockading Toulon, she received some 87½ tons of water, 11 live bullocks, 5,730 pounds of onions and 2,070 lemons from the *Isabella* transport. The log also states that she continued to replenish from the *Prevoyant* storeship between 16 and 30 August and that during this period she also received "5 bullocks, six bags of Onions and One bag of cabbage" from the 74-gun ship *Belleisle*. *Victory* also transferred a cask containing 1,400 lemons over to the 74-gun ship *Canopus*.

Issuing Food

Food was issued to the crew from the ship steward's room, a space partitioned from the bread room, which contained bins called "rundels", each of which held the ready-to-use provisions and a counter on which the steward would measure out the rations. The steward worked directly for the purser and, because he lived next to the bread room, which also contained flour, he was nicknamed "Jack-of-the-Dust", later shortened to "Jack Dusty", the modern sailor's name for any naval stores cleric. The day's ration was issued to each "mess cook", who was responsible for preparing the food for his own mess before taking it to the ship's cook in the galley. Once the food was cooked, the mess cook retrieved his mess rations and served it up to his mess mates. Most messes comprised four to six men, not the larger groups many people wrongly imagine. There were three mealtimes a day for the crew. Breakfast, at 8 a.m., was generally an oatmeal gruel, which was sometimes sweetened with molasses, later with sugar. Dinner, at noon, was served to the entire ship's company, leaving the bare minimum of personnel on deck keeping watch. This was done for two reasons: to make at least one part of the day a group social occasion, thereby helping to uphold morale, and to minimize the length of time the galley fires were lit, to conserve fuel. Dinner comprised meat (pork or beef) boiled with peas, oatmeal or other vegetables. Supper, served at 4 p.m., generally consisted of ship's biscuit with either butter or cheese.

In heavy rolling seas, cooking on the open part of the galley fire hearth was precarious; likewise it was easy to spill victuals contained in the mess kid.

Typical mess scene at sea showing sailors relaxing with their beer or grog, singing songs or telling stories. Mess equipment and kit bags are stowed in the background.

Drink

Drink for the ship's company consisted of rum, beer and wine, depending on availability and the location in which the ship was operating. On the whole, rum – generally referred to as "grog" – was issued twice daily, at dinner and at supper time, the daily ration being diluted one part rum to two parts water to prevent drunkenness. Before the 1740s, rum, at a measure of half a pint, had been issued as an alternative to beer in the West Indies because of its availability and because it was falsely believed to prevent scurvy. Unfortunately issuing very strong rum to ships' crews resulted in drunkenness and incompetence. Disturbed by the escalating problem, Admiral Edward Vernon, then Commander-in-Chief of the West Indies decided that the rum ration should be diluted. On 21 August 1740 he issued an order stating that the daily ration of rum be diluted with one quart (2 pints) of water and that it was "to be mixed in a scuttle butt kept for that purpose, and to be done upon the deck, and in the presence of the lieutenant of the watch, who is to take particular care to see that the men are not defrauded in having their full allowance of rum, and when so mixed it is to be served to them in two servings in the day, the one between 10 and 12 in the morning, and the other between 4 and 6 in the afternoon." In time, Vernon's decree became standard throughout the British fleet, and because he often wore a "grogram" coat and was affectionately nicknamed "old grogram", the term "grog" soon became common for the diluted rum issue. If rum could not be procured, brandy was occasionally issued as an alternative. By the early 1800s, lemon or lime juice was often mixed with the rum to prevent scurvy.

Each man could receive a daily ration of up to eight pints of beer, which was issued as a substitute for water because it kept better at sea. Although the quantity given appears high, this was "small beer" of relatively low alcoholic content. Generally brewed within the Royal Victualling Yards, Portsmouth's yard being the best for quality, beer was mainly supplied to the ships of the Channel fleet and home waters. On the North American station, spruce beer was also acquired as an alternative to common beer. Wine was issued as a substitute to beer for ships serving in the Mediterranean, where supplies were plentiful, with each man receiving two pints daily. The *Vanguard*, for example, laying off Naples in July 1799 embarked 20 pipes (2,152 gallons) of wine before sailing and when at Port Mahon four weeks later received 15 pipes (2,115 gallons) of wine.

Officers' Food

While the purser was responsible for maintaining the ship's standard provisions, officers could and did supply alternative foodstuffs in order to supplement their own diets. Chickens, which of course provided eggs as well as meat, quails and ducks, were kept in coops up on the deck and it was not unusual to find goats and pigs which were kept on board as well. In addition to livestock, the officers brought on board personal supplies of packed provisions, preserved hams and tongues being a particular favourite.

Admirals, who were often obliged to host diplomats and other officers on board ship, would take an immense quantity of packed food to sea for this purpose. The procurement list compiled for the Earl of St. Vincent (formerly Admiral Sir John Jervis) at Portsmouth on 28 February 1806, for example, comprised the following number of delicacies: almonds, allspice, black and white pepper, candy capers, cayenne, chilli vinegar, cloves, celery seeds, cinnamon, currants, curry powder, elder vinegar, essence of anchovies, French olives, Harvey's sauce, Hyson tea, India soy, India ketchup, Isinglass, Jamaica ginger, lemon pickle, mace, macaroni, milk chocolate, mixed pickles, morels, muscatels, mushrooms, nutmegs, oil, pearl barley, pickled cabbage, pickled cucumbers, pickled onions, pickled walnuts, Quins sauce, raisins, rice, side bacon, spirits of wine, Souchong tea, sugar loaves, tarragon vinegar, Turkish coffee, truffles and vermicelli!

An officer's store chest.

General Supplies and Stores

Besides food, water and other provisions required to sustain the crew, the ships needed regular supplies of military hardware in order to maintain themselves in a state of constant readiness for combat. As was the case with the general provisions, this type of equipment could either be

Solid iron cannon shot being manufactured and graded at Woolwich Arsenal.

supplied directly from the naval dockyards at home or from foreign bases, such as Antigua, Gibraltar, Halifax, Madras and Bombay, to name but a few. Such stores were supplied by transport ships, which could either deliver the stock to the various naval bases or alternatively transfer it directly to the vessels themselves. Much of this equipment was needed to replenish stores consumed by ships' boatswains, carpenters and gunners. For example, the frigate *La Minerve* (originally French), laying at anchor at Porto Ferrejo, Elba, on 4 October 1796 embarked stores for the boatswain which comprised: "3 barrels of Tar 20 Yards of Kersey [course woollen cloth] 4 Log Lines 36 lbs Twine 6 lbs tread and 66 oars." That same day the carpenter was to receive: "1 Deep Sea Lead Lines, 2 Logs Do., 40 lbs tallow, 40 Block Pins and 9 lbs Yellow Paint." Much larger items, such as roughed down masts and spars, were also provided, as well as timber, pitch and oil for paint. The logbook of the *Vanguard* for 7 July 1808 records that while laying at anchor in Helsinborg Roads she received the following boatswain's and carpenter's stores from the 16 gun sloops *Tartarus* and *Ranger*:

Boatswain's stores:

1 five-inch cablet, 120 fathoms in length
429 yards of canvas
1 eight-inch stream cable
1 four-inch cablet
1 hawser, 338 fathoms in length
1 deep sea line
4 white hides
12 graplin [sic] irons
24 blocks
32 pounds of twine

Carpenter's stores:

28 gallons and 3 quarts of black varnish
40 feet of wainscot
13 feet of half-inch thick elm
15 feet of one-inch-thick pine
20 feet of half-inch deal
20 pounds of spikes and wrought nails
218 pound of standard nails
28 leather scuppers
29 white plates of tin
1 barrel of varnish

Note: Rope sizes given above refer to their circumference; i.e. the eight-inch stream cable would be two and a half inches thick.

In addition to the warrant officer's stores, the domestic requirements of a ship also had to be maintained – coal and wood for the galley fire, replacement hammocks and bedding etc. The *Vanguard*'s logbooks of 1808 can be used as an example: she transferred 150 flock beds (mattresses) into a transport for the troops being sent on shore and two weeks later received 100 hammocks from the sloop *Tartarus* for her own crew. Besides the many instances of embarking hammocks, the logbooks also show that boxes of candles, bales of slop clothing comprising shirts, frocks, trousers and stockings and cases of shoes and hats, were also regularly supplied to ships while they were stationed on active duty. Candles, hammocks, bedding, clothing and shoes were retained by the purser who, with the exception of the candles, sold these items to the seamen when required.

Health and Medical Care

Keeping the entire ship's crew in good heath was essential for running a man o' war efficiently. Men needed to be fit to operate the rigging and sails, to man the yards aloft, and – most importantly – to be able to fight when brought into action. Sea battles at this period were not won by good ship handling, seamanship and gunnery alone, but by keeping the crew healthy. Health could be maintained only by providing a nutritious diet (albeit high in calories), the introduction of preventative medicine and by establishing good hygiene practices. As Nelson himself said: "The great thing in all military service is health and you will agree with me that it is easier for an officer to keep men healthy, than for a physician to cure them."

At the beginning of the wars with France in 1793, some 42 per cent of deaths within the Georgian navy were caused by disease, whereas an average of only three to five per cent were killed in battle. This does not mean that higher casualties could not be sustained in action, it all very much depended on the ferocity of the engagement – when attacking Fort Moultrie on 28 June 1776, 11 per cent of the *Bristol*'s crew were killed. At Trafalgar, the *Victory*, which had the highest number of British casualties, had seven per cent of its crew killed, while the *Prince*, also present at the same battle, suffered none.

Death from accidents appear to have been extraordinarily low, especially when one considers the frequency with which large numbers of men had to work aloft. While most falls from the rigging incurred serious injuries, it is remarkable that on average only one man died annually on each ship from such an occurrence. Such a reality is supported by Captain Berry when writing to his father-in-law in May 1798. After enduring a terrible storm off Genoa while commanding the *Vanguard*, Berry wrote: "Before 12 at night the gale came on, and increased with rapid violence, which obliged us to furl all the sails and try under a main storm-staysail. At about two, the main-topmast went over the side, with the top-sail yard full of men. I dreaded the inquiry of who were killed and drowned; fortunately only one man fell overboard, and one fell on the booms, and was killed on the spot."

The majority of injuries or deaths were caused either by common misfortune or by accidents generated by the ship's motion in heavy seas – men falling down ladders, being thrown against parts of the ship's fittings, or ship's boats being overturned. Hernias, caused by lifting extremely heavy weights without mechanical aids, were very common, and seamen who suffered from such an injury were issued with trusses. Other injuries at sea were usually caused through simple neglect or ignorance. A man accidentally falling overboard was quite a common occurence and, although it is believed that most sailors could not swim, about 35 per cent of those that went into the sea were recovered alive. Should the victim have partially drowned, the surgeon would treat him by administering a strong onion broth, which helped prevent bronchitis or other inflammatory lung problems from developing.

Death through suicide in the Georgian navy was extremely rare. The one isolated case found relates to a seaman named William Maynard who "was found hanging in the bread room" on board the *Albemarle* on Sunday 18 March 1781. Unfortunately, the logbook provides no clue as to why Maynard took his life; more tragic is the fact that this incident occurred at Woolwich after the ship had returned home from the West Indies. Death by suicide was not, however, a common event in Georgian society.

Because warships of this period were densely populated, with most of the crew confined to living on one deck, the major problem that faced naval surgeons was dealing with disease, which, if not isolated, could sweep through the ship and devastate the entire crew. In home waters, the concern lay with typhus. The most significant problems, however, arose when a ship was operating in tropical climates, where malaria, yellow fever, tropical sprue and other debilitating disorders were rife. With exception to malaria, all these diseases are gastro-intestinal infections, causing diarrhoea and consequently dehydration, fever, melancholy and weakness.

The speed with which these diseases could reduce a crew are made clear in the logbooks of Nelson's ship *Hinchingbroke*. On assuming command from Nelson on 1 May 1780, *Hinchingbroke*'s new commander, Captain Cuthbert Collingwood, wrote: "The ship is very leaky, and 70 men with fevers: John Stockbridge departed this life." To make matters worse, the surgeon's mate, James Hugggins, died the next day. Between 1 May and 8 September, Collingwood was to lose 124 men out of a crew of around 200. To overcome the problem, fit seamen were sent on shore to erect tents into which the sick were removed. Following this, the *Hinchingbroke*'s surgeon set about getting the crew to wash the ship with vinegar – vinegar being used as a disinfectant. They also fumigated the ship by setting up "fire in iron pots continuously burning on the lower deck", each of which would have contained brimstone (sulphur). So debilitated were the *Hinchingbroke*'s crew that seamen from accompanying ships undertook getting water and wood, and later assisted in sailing the ship back to Port Royal, Jamaica.

The epidemic on board the *Elephant* while anchored at Spithead in October 1790

A scene below decks showing a man having his leg amputated. This is an anonymous graphite drawing circa 1820.

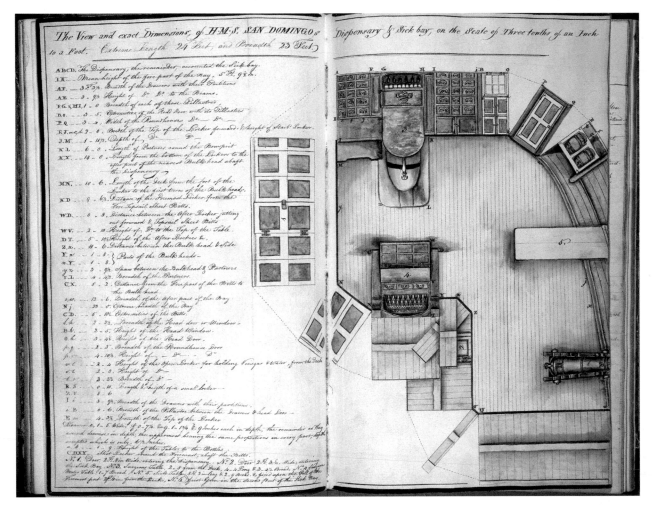

Left: Diagram of the sick berth fitted under the forecastle of the 74-gun ship San Domingo in 1812 taken from Captain S. J. Pechell's journal. It shows the dispensary, operating table fitted over a gun, door to the heads (toilets) and portable bulkheads. This sick berth would be dismantled in battle to allow operation of the guns.

Below left: This surgeon's medical chest holds up to 30 medicine bottles, which would have contained various powders and liquids to meet all manner of ailments.

also clarifies what measures surgeons undertook to treat viruses. Although it is unclear from Captain Thompson's logbook what disease was prevalent within the ship – in all probability it was typhus – it does show that 11 per cent of the crew found infected were removed from the ship directly into the naval hospital at Haslar within the first week. His journal also clearly describes the orderly procedure of dealing with disease-ridden ships. The first measures taken were to move the *Elephant* alongside the hulk *Goliath*, a redundant ship out of commission used for

accommodation, before undertaking a systematic procedure to eliminate all sources of the problem. While more men were sent to hospital, the remaining crew methodically washed the ship throughout with vinegar and fumigated each deck using tobacco smoke as an alternative to burning brimstone or gunpowder. To do this effectively, all gun ports had to be shut. All potential sources of disease – filthy shingle ballast was often the cause of fever – was heaved out of the *Elephant* during this cleaning process. As for the men, all were systematically removed, mess by mess, into the *Goliath*, where they could be thoroughly washed without contamination and have their clothes fumigated with tobacco. In all, 146 men, which represented some 27 per cent of the *Elephant*'s crew, had been sent into Haslar.

The advances that had been made in naval medicine by the end of the 18th century were greatly influenced by three physicians, Sir Gilbert Blane, James Lind and Thomas Trotter, all well-experienced and respected practitioners. Under their leadership, naval surgeons had acquired a far better understanding of disease and prevention. Moreover, initiatives were also taken up by ships' commanders to assist them in combating the problem of contagion. With the exception of a few cases during the Seven Years' War, it had long been the practice to move the sick to one separate area of the deck where the main body of the crew lived, with the result that the infection continued to spread. The first documented attempt to provide better facilities for tending to the sick is attributed to Captain John Markham of the 74-gun ship *Centaur*, which was serving with the Mediterranean fleet in 1798 under the command of Admiral Sir John Jervis (Earl St.Vincent). Markham moved his sick berth from the lower deck to an area on the upper gun deck under the starboard side of the forecastle. This space, 19 feet in length and covering the room of two gun ports, was bounded at the centreline by the ship's galley and iron Brodie stove. The entire area, regarded as a ward, contained some 22 beds or cradles. At the foremost end of the ward, adjacent to the transverse beakhead bulkhead was a dispensary eight feet in length. This dispensary, complete with a medicine cupboard and a table, served as a daily facility only; the main dispensary was situated down below on the orlop beside the surgeon's cabin. Placing the sick berth under the forecastle provided many advantages for aiding the recovery of men:

1. There was plenty of light and fresh air.
2. Having a segregated toilet facility located within the beakhead bulkhead prevented contagion from being transferred from the sick to the healthy crew members.
3. Being near the galley Brodie stove, there was a plentiful supply of both hot water and heat. Hot broth could be easily administered to the ill.

Welcoming Markham's concept, Admiral Sir John Jervis issued the following directive to his fleet: "The Commander in Chief positively directs that no sick are to kept below the upper deck in any line of battle ship under his command, and that a sick berth is to be prepared in each [ship] under the forescastel on the starboard side with a roundhouse enclosed for the sick." (The roundhouse was an enclosed toilet or "head".) While adhered to, this order met with some criticism, because livestock had to be moved elsewhere to accommodate the sick berth. One ship complained that the removal of their hog-sty caused "the swine to range the main deck to the annoyance of the men".

Following Markham's example, segregated sick berths were introduced to the ships of the Channel fleet in 1799–1800 and were formally introduced throughout the entire fleet by a Navy Board Order in 1801. Though following the ideas of Sir Gilbert Blane, Markham's concept could very well have been formulated by the fact that he had commanded the *Hinchingbroke* after Collingwood. Although he was credited with the official change of the location of the sick berth, the idea was not entirely new. John Knyverton, a surgeon's mate who served during the Seven Years' War, recalls in his memoirs, *The Surgeon's Mate*, that the sick berth in his ship was sited under the forecastle.

Apart from treating tropical disease, daily injuries, common aliments and venereal disease, ship's surgeons also had to cope with battle casualties. It is commonly imagined that surgeons and their assistants spent their entire time in action carrying out endless amputation operations. What is often forgotten is that battle casualties comprised a host of wound types: injuries caused by missiles and bullets, splinter penetration wounds, burns and compound fractures, as well as concussion and shock. Working under extreme conditions and with little assistance, the naval surgeon had to be methodical and expedient in both assessing the severity of each injury presented to him, and resolving its cure, all the while remaining impartial to the status of the victim, the cries of the wounded and dying around him and the noise of the battle above. He also had to decide which casualties would benefit from operation and which would die anyway. When Nelson was fatally wounded at Trafalgar, for example, Dr. Beatty knew that he was beyond help and Nelson was therefore made as comfortable as possible before his death. As today, the surgeon accepted the fact that most abdominal wounds were generally fatal, thus comfort and compassion were all that could be offered, whilst the ship's chaplain assisted in his time-honoured way.

Missile injuries included those caused by round shot, chain and bar shot, grape shot, musket and pistol shot. Being smaller, musket and pistol balls could, if they had not shattered the bone, be removed using specially designed extractors, the ball being held by the muscles surrounding it going into spasm. It was the weight and velocity of the larger projectiles that inflicted the most horrendous wounds. Besides decapitating or taking off the limbs of victims, these projectiles often simply sliced away portions of flesh and muscle from the victim or shattered their bones, and it was these cases that presented surgeons with the most disconcerting problems. In those instances where only the flesh had been removed, the surgeon could do little but staunch the bleeding and stitch the casualty together as best he could. The alternative solution was amputation, and because of the number of compound fractures and traumatic avulsions (i.e. severing of limbs) that occurred, naval surgeons were experts in this form of operation. Most were capable of performing a complete amputation operation with great dexterity within two minutes.

Most amputations involved the following procedure: time permitting, the skin was washed and shaved beforehand, after which the patient was anaesthetized with laudanum or morphine and given a wad of leather to bite on. The practice of anaesthetizing the victim with rum or other spirits, as commonly believed, was actually avoided, because alcohol thins the blood, which prevents it from clotting. If the operation was to be successful, it was essential that the blood would clot, otherwise the patient could bleed to death. Tourniquets were then applied, which provided temporary anaesthesia localized to the limb. The surgeon made a circular cut around the limb, below the wound, peeling back the resultant flap of skin above the point of amputation. Using either an amputation saw or a knife, he then cut though the bone. Next the tourniquets were eased and bleeding blood vessels were clinched with forceps while the surgeon applied sutures to seal all blood vessels. With this complete, the flap of skin was stitched over to close the stump and the entire wound was sealed with oil of turpentine – not boiling tar as is commonly believed. After the operation the victim would be given more laudanum or morphine to ease the trauma as the original anaesthetic wore off, but as these items were invaluable, a draught of spirits or wine to ease the pain would have been more common.

Although singular amputations were common, one surgeon, Ralph Cumming, successfully undertook the first ever forequarter amputation in the naval hospital at Antigua in 1808. His patient had had his arm torn away at the shoulder by a round shot from a fort at Guadaloupe, and the injuries were so extensive that Cumming was obliged to remove the remains of the arm together with the collar bone and shoulder blade. This was a highly complicated operation, demanding an expert knowledge of anatomy, and involved suturing many blood vessels. Although terribly scarred, the sailor made a full recovery and later reported to Greenwich Hospital to claim his pension. Cumming was not so fortunate – he died shortly afterwards from yellow fever.

Splinter wounds resulting from "ragged fragments of timber violently rent from the planks or sides of the ship" by round shot were common. According to surgeon Alexander Hutchison, "wounds inflicted by splinters of wood are always more extensive, accompanied with frightful contusions and lacerations of the soft parts." Splinters were generally removed using probes after removing the skin with a fleam (a razor-edged flaying knife) and the wound was then sewn up. Badly lacerated splinter wounds often resulted in amputation, as this was often quicker than attempting to cure the limb. The major problem deriving from splinter wounds was tetanus, therefore all foreign matter had to be removed with probes before infection could take hold.

Penetration wounds, caused by pikes, cutlasses, bayonets and hatchets, were dealt with according to the severity of the wound or its proximity to internal organs. While wounds caused by the former three weapons were generally confined to the torso and arms, hatchet wounds mainly affected the head, face and shoulders. Whatever the injury, the main objective was to stop the haemorrhaging either by suture or by pressure bandaging. Where internal bleeding could not be stemmed, it was customary to lower blood pressure by blood letting to allow the blood to clot.

Right: Admiral Sir John Jervis, Earl St. Vincent. Jervis introduced many reforms into the navy, including proper sick berths.

Fire and explosion presented a far greater hazard to the ships and men of the Nelsonian period than did round shot. Irrespective of the fact that immense precautions were undertaken to confine gunpowder within the magazines, cartridges conveyed to the guns during battle could easily be ignited and the resultant explosions and flash-fires could cause scorching to men. One common source of burns came from firing guns using slowmatch: although the match was held at a distance with a linstock, the flash from the powder spread at the touch hole could prove risky. Because this kind of wound affected some 25 per cent of gunners, surgeons, as well as gunnery officers, campaigned for the introduction of flint-operated gunlocks. As a result, the incidence of flash burns caused by firing virtually disappeared. Burns were generally treated by applying linseed oil; the alternative was to use urine, which is sterile.

When going into battle, the surgeon went to his station down below in the dim confines of the orlop, or onto a platform within

the hold if he was on a frigate, and prepared an emergency operating theatre and reception for receiving the wounded. Assisting him were the surgeon's mates, loblolly boys, the chaplain, the purser, valets and other non-combatants. Possibly donned in a black smock or leather apron used at the time, he laid out his surgical instruments – amputation saws and knives, torniquets, fleams and probes to removes splinters, bullet extractors, ligatures to bind arteries, needles and sutures to stitch up wounds, forceps and tweezers. His assistants placed out buckets for "wings and limbs", water for washing wounds and surgical instruments and tore up linen for bandages. Vinegar was used as a disinfectant and oil of turpentine to seal limb stubs (tar was used only as a last resort). Canvas and bedding was spread along the wings of the orlop for the wounded to lie on while awaiting the services of the surgeon. Although naval surgeons could deal with most injuries caused by accident or battle, they had no antibiotics to tackle infection. It was not uncommon, therefore, to find that some patients died after successful operations, irrespective of the surgeon's skill. It was during aftercare that many problems surfaced: men died from loss of blood, as a result of being traumatized by pain, or they simply lost their will to live. Every endeavour was made to transfer wounded men off the ship at the earliest opportunity, either to hospital ships that operated with each major squadron, or to one of the various on-shore naval hospitals.

Above: "The Death of Nelson" by Arthur Devis. This painting clearly shows the dim confines of the orlop where battle casualties were taken. When the Victory *returned to England, Devis spent three weeks on board preparing sketches to produce this masterpiece. The original remains on board the* Victory *at Portsmouth.*

1.	2.	3.	4.	5.	6.
DUTCH	7.	8.	9.	0.	

Alphabetical

A	B	C	D	E	F
G	H	I	K	L	M
N	O	P	Q	R	S
T	U	V	W	X	Y

INTELLIGENCE, ESPIONAGE AND SIGNALLING

Most intelligence was gathered by the smaller ships of the frigates classes and below. Being of shallower draught, they could travel close inshore to undertake reconnaissance work of enemy coastal installations and fortifications, as well as naval shipping at anchor. Information was also obtained by stopping and questioning neutral merchant ships that visited enemy ports. Fishing vessels similarly proved to be a useful source of acquiring data. On many occasions warships would be ordered to convey government agents who were on special missions, landing them on foreign shores to gather information or to rendezvous with royalist sympathizers.

View of the telegraph erected on the Admiralty Office in February 1796.

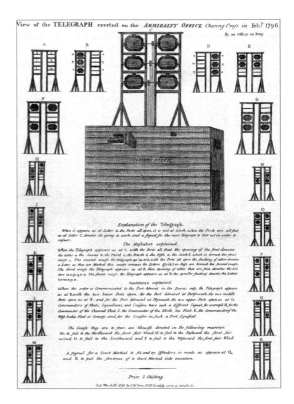

Nelson's famous signal "England expects..." is prepared and hoisted on the mizzen mast of the Victory *under the supervision of Lieutenant John Pasco.*

By far the best way of finding out information about enemies and their movements, however, was by capturing their ships. These ships may well have been carrying despatches, special documents, letters and orders, all of which would provide vital clues to the strength and political intentions of the enemy. Not only that, the capture of an enemy ship brought in prize money. It is highly probable that most senior officers had some ability in reading, if not speaking, the language of the enemy, just as the enemy in all likelihood would have been able to understand English. In such cases captured documents could be quickly translated. Ships carrying personnel who had linguistic skills, irrespective of their rank, would have particular advantage. One such person was Nelson's chaplain and confidential secretary, the Reverend Alexander John Scott. Scott, a scholar in French, Spanish and Italian, used his language skills to assist Nelson in arranging the Convention of Copenhagen in 1801. Scott would often go on shore in the guise of a scholar seeking antiquarian books, all the while reading newspapers and eavesdropping on conversations, which often provided invaluable intelligence. On board ship he would decipher captured despatches and letters. Men like Scott, however, were rare.

Records show that British warships carried foreign ensigns, which often proved useful in creating a ruse, especially when the ship needed to get close inshore. Enemy signal books were of vital importance; not only could they help to read messages sent by enemy ships, but, conversely, false signals could be sent to confuse the enemy.

Signals were vital for effective communication between ships in the fleet, ship-to-shore transmission and relaying messages and order from the Admiralty based at Whitehall to the various fleets stationed along the south coast. Ship-to-ship and ship-to-shore communication was mainly achieved by using coloured flags flown from specific masts of the ship during daylight. At night, signalling was restricted to the use of groups of coloured lanthorns, and signal guns were used in fog and during other inclement conditions.

Over the years the signalling codes employed became more intricate as the system was remodelled and improved by consecutive admirals to meet a wider range of messages and instructions for manoeuvring a fleet in battle. Added to this were a host of instructions that assisted the daily requirements of a fleet, even to the point that one ship could acknowledge that it could provide another with a spare anchor. Although the code had been improved by Admiral Kempenfelt in about 1780 and extended by Admiral Howe at the beginning of the war with France in 1793, the code introduced by Admiral Sir Home Popham in 1800, and its revision in 1803, became most widely recognized, largely due to its connection with Nelson's famous signal at Trafalgar, "England expects that every men will do his duty." Popham changed his code in 1803 after the French captured a British ship together with its signal book, which, normally contained in a lead-weighted bag, failed to be thrown overboard before capture.

Popham's Telegraphic Code of 1803 remained in use for the remainder of the war until 1814. The code contained ten separate identifiable signal flags together with preparative and acknowledgement pendants – flags were rectangular in shape, pendants triangular. The ten signal flags were numbered nought to nine, therefore any combination of numbers could be created, providing that each ship carried at least eight sets of the ten primary flags. Signals could thus be sent under a numbered form that related to either specific messages or words within the signal book, which contained as many as 6,000 words or established useful phrases. In addition, the ten numbers also represented letters of the alphabet, which enabled individual words to be sent using groups of numbers.

Flag number	Letter	Flag number(s)	Letter	Flag numbers	Letter	Flag numbers	Letter	Flag numbers	Letter
1	A	6	F	11	L	16	Q	21	V
2	B	7	G	12	M	17	R	22	W
3	C	8	H	13	N	18	S	23	X
4	D	9	I & J	14	O	19	T	24	Y
5	E	10	K	15	P	20	U	25	Z

NOTE: At the time the letter J was not yet fully recognised a part of the alphabet.

Nelson's last signal flown at the battle of Trafalgar, phrased as "engage the enemy more closely", was simply represented by two flags, numbers one and six, giving the signal code number 16. Up to four numbers could be used to specify a single word or instructional phrase: the word England comprised three flags producing the number 253; Expects was 269; That – 463; Every – 261; Man – 471; Will – 958; Do – 220; and His – 370. The word duty was not specified in the code, however, so had to be spelt out using a total of seven flags.

Other signals, such as "Shall I leave off action?", or simply the word "action", consisted of four flags producing the number 2026. A more mundane matter, such as "I cannot spare an anchor stock", or just "anchor stock", was number 2045 – it was all a question of interpretation by the

Signals used by Lord Nelson at the battle of Trafalgar, 21 October 1805.

experienced signal officer. All he had to do was read each set of flags from top to bottom and look up the corresponding number in the code book. All signal flags were housed in special lockers fitted on the poop deck, or on the quarter deck on frigates, each of which comprised some 80 pigeon holes to contain four sets of numbered flags and pendants.

Besides inter-ship communication using signal flags, an intricate, land-based semaphore system was set up in 1796 under Lord George Murray to provide communication direct from the Admiralty at Whitehall to the various fleet anchorages centred around the southern and eastern coast. At first there were only two communication routes: one running south to Portsmouth, where communication could be made to the fleet anchored at Spithead and St. Helen's, the other going east to Deal and subsequently to the squadrons laying in the Downs. This eastern network also divided off at Gads Hill, one leg going to Chatham, the other to Sheerness where the fleet lay in wait at the Nore. In 1806, the network to Portsmouth was extended west from Beacon Hill towards Plymouth and the fleet in the Hamoaze, and finally, in 1808, a third network going north east to (Great) Yarmouth in Norfolk was added. This communication system comprised a chain of telegraph stations built at set distances upon suitable hill tops along the route, each station being manned by a lieutenant and a retired seaman. When fully completed in 1808, the entire network embraced a total of 63 telegraph stations. The actual telegraph apparatus consisted of six shutters mounted on a large frame, the shutters being operated by ropes. When not in use, all shutters were left open; i.e. in the horizontal plane, and when ready to transmit, they were all closed (vertical). Although totally reliant on good visibility, signals could be passed from the Admiralty in London to Portsmouth in about ten minutes.

In addition to the Admiralty telegraph network there was also a host of signal stations dotted along the entire length of the southern and eastern coastline to provide ship-to-shore communication. These stations also proved useful for warning merchant ships of potential danger of approaching enemy vessels. Set up in 1795, these signalling posts – 65 in total – extended from Rame Head just west of Plymouth to Great Yarmouth in Norfolk, with a further 81 stations around the Irish coast. Each station had a mast and gaff yard on which semaphore flags were flown, together with spherical balls to make up the required signal. In addition, each was equipped with a union flag, two red flags of differing size, one white flag, red, white and blue pendants and 12 signal balls. There was a frame for hoisting lanthorns for night communication.

BIBLIOGRAPHY

PRIMARY SOURCES (Public Record Office, Kew)
ADM 51 Series: Captain's Log Books
ADM 52 Series: Master's Log Book
ADM 160 Series: Ordnance Records

SECONDARY SOURCES
Beresford, Lord C. and Wilson, H. W., *Nelson and his Times*, 12 parts (London 1897–1898).

Bryant, A., *The Years of Endurance 1793–1802* (London 1944).

Bryant, A., *The Years of Victory 1803–1812* (London 1944).

Callander, G., *The Story of HMS Victory* (London 1914).

Clowes, W. L., *The Royal Navy: A History from the Earliest Times to 1900*, 7 vols (London 1996/7).

Gardiner, R., *Fleet, Battle and Blockade: The French Revolutionary War 1793–1797* (London 1996).

Gardiner R., *Nelson against Napoleon: From the Nile to Copenhagen 1798–1801* (London 1996).

Gardiner, R., *The Campaign of Trafalgar 1803–1805* (London 1996).

Glover, R., *Britain at Bay: Defence against Bonaparte, 1803–1814* (London 1973).

Goodwin P., *The Construction and Fitting of the Sailing Man of War 1650–1850* (London 1987).

Goodwin P., *The 20 Gun Ship Blandford 1719* (London 1988).

Goodwin P., *The Bomb Vessel Granado 1742* (London 1989).

Goodwin P., *The Naval Cutter Alert 1777* (London 1991).

Goodwin P., *Countdown to Victory: 101 Questions and Answers about HMS Victory* (Portsmouth 2000).

Goodwin P., *Nelson's Ships: A History of the Vessels in which he Served 1771–1805* (London 2002).

Goodwin P., "The Development of the Sick Berth, 1740–1815", *Journal of the Royal Naval Medical Service*, vol.36, no 2.

HMS Vanguard at the Nile, the men, the ship, the battle (Nelson Society 1998).

HMS Elephant (Nelson Society 2001).

James, W. M., *The History of Great Britain from the Declaration of War by France in 1793 to the Accession of George IV. A New Edition with Additions and Notes*, 6 vols (London 1837).

James, W. M., *The British Navy in Adversity* (London 1926).

Lavery, B., *The Arming and Fitting of English Ships of War 1600–1815*, (London 1987).

Lavery, B., *The Naval War against Napoleon* (London 1998).

Lavery B., *Shipboard Life and Organisation 1731–1815* (Navy Records Society 1998).

Lavery B., *Nelson's Navy* (London rp 2000).

Lewis, M., *A Social History of the Royal Navy 1793–1815* (London 1960).

Lyon, D., *The Sailing Navy List* (London 1993).

Oman, C., *Nelson* (London 1947).

Schom, A., *Trafalgar, Countdown to Battle, 1803–1805* (London 1990).

Southey, R., *The Life of Horatio Lord Nelson* (London 1906).

Tracy, N., *Nelson's Battles* (London 1996).

Tracy, N., (Ed) *The Naval Chronicle: The Contemporary Record of the Royal Navy at War*, 5 vols (London 1999, consolidated edition).

Wilkinson-Latham, R., *British Artillery on Land and Sea: 1790–1820* (Newton Abbott 1973).

White, C., *1797, Nelson's Year of Destiny* (Sutton 1998).

Woodman, R., *The Victory of Seapower: Winning the War against Napoleon, 1806–1814* (London 1997).